I0553374

FARM ANIMALS

ASH ERICMORE

D & T
PUBLISHING

FARM
ANIMALS

C H A P T E R 1

His fingers had been curled to a fist for some time. A couple of hours, maybe. It was hard to tell. Damage to the nerves? Matt didn't know. It hurt like hell though. Like a cramp. He shivered. Sitting on the ground amid the dirt and straw. Looking at the metal clasp around his wrist.

The walls of the barn closing in. Always closing in.

He breathed in deeply. He could smell the animals. They weren't making any noise yet. Through the cracks in the wooden walls, daylight, but if the animals were quiet—they hadn't even screamed for food yet—it must still be early morning. He leaned his head back against the wall behind him. The cool of the damp wood penetrated his matted hair. Made him shiver more. He tried to straighten his legs out in front of him. The left did. The right, not so much. He was sure his knee was straight, but the leg... broken. He thought it had healed like that. Refixed itself under the skin. It didn't hurt anymore. Not like it had at the time.

One of the cows was moving in the stall to the right of him. He could hear it stumbling about like it had just awoken. He considered that they were standing up when asleep. Never thought about it before. He wanted to say that he'd look it up when he got home, but he was pretty sure he wasn't going home.

Not now.

He didn't know how long he'd been there, weeks, maybe months. His leg—Anton had broken it. He'd beaten Matt—tied up, he recalled—and then pushed his leg over something. It was all a bit of a blur. Then he'd stomped him. Like *curb stomped,* but with the leg. The snapping sound had cut through the quiet of the basement. He remembered the basement. It was warm. Dry. Some days he'd been able to smell the cooking in the house above. The food was enticing. Used to drive him wild. That was before he'd become lame. Put out in the barn with the rest of the animals. He shook his head. Out here. He was dying. Probably from exposure. He blinked it away.

Yeah. How long? The healing process on the leg must have been weeks. At least two or three. And that wasn't all of it. Shit. He wrapped his arms around himself. He tried to rub some warmth into his bones.

The cow moved again and the guttural noise of it moaning for breakfast came. The others would start soon enough.

It was getting colder in the mornings, too. Only a little, but spending all day and night out there, you could tell. His toes wouldn't move properly now. He wondered if that was—

A sudden chorus of cow noise rose. Breakfast time.

At first, he thought it was the sound of the cows that brought the food, but he'd since realised that the sound of the cows was because they knew the food was coming. It was either that they could hear him. Or they could sense it. Some sort of bovine sixth sense. Not that his newfound insight into the working of cow brains was going to do him any good.

He looked across the dirt. So, *he* would be here in a minute.

He rolled to the side and slipped down into the dirt in a foetal position. He'd hoped that pretending to be asleep he would be left alone, but it hadn't. Not so far. Hope. That was about all he had left.

The door opened on the other side of the barn. The light cast new shadows out to the corner that Matt lived in. He curled tighter.

He made strange noises as he fed the cows in the barn. Three of them, Matt thought. Strange, clicking noises. Then the words, "Get'in' big, aye?" came from across the other side. Maybe one of the cows was pregnant? Maybe that was why they were kept in there?

Matt opened his eyes. Laying on the ground, he could see beneath the wall of the stall. All the cows up and milling about, he could see *his* feet. Entrenched in wellies covered in shit. A bucket dropped carefully to the straw at his feet.

Matt lowered his eyes, pulling them tightly closed.

He waited. Hoping. Praying, that *he* wouldn't do anything. Pleading to a god he now believed in. A horrible vengeful god. One who punished him with wrath. For that was the only explanation that Matt could conjure for what had happened to him.

The sound of the man moving. *He* was standing there. Over Matt. He could *feel* him there.

"No youse pretending," he said.

Matt opened his eyes. It could have been a test. Wouldn't have mattered, would it? He looked up at the man, standing over him. He was wearing those jeans he wore to do the farm work and that dark green jacket. Looked like an old person's puffer jacket. Flat cap. The most unassuming British farmer. He had his shotgun. It was open over his arm like he was striding the fields about to shoot pheasant or call for the clay pigeon to be released.

"No good to me," he said, shaking his head. "Such a shame." He snapped the gun shut, it clacking into place. He held it like a baby, cradled in his arms.

Matt grunted out words as best he could. His tongue had long gone to the wind.

"Eh? What's that?" he said. Then he started laughing. "Oh, you," he said. "I don't know what to do wit' you. I want to keep you, but youse not producing anymore. Youse not …" he paused, thinking for the right words, "… fis-cal-ly vi-a-ble."

Fiscally viable. Matt eyed the gun. *He* twisted it in his arms and pointed it at Matt. He curled tighter on the ground. Sounds eeking from his mouth as he tried to plead for his life. Desperate noises drooling from him as piss slipped into the straw.

All silent in the barn, except for the chewing of the feed. The shuffle of hooves.

He sniffed snot up, and Matt opened his eyes. Looked at the man. Standing there. Gun pointing. He looked sad. He stopped and turned away. "I don't know if I can do it," he muttered into the shadows. "I don't … know."

The last of the piss drained from Matt and he tried to sit up right, his back hunched over. He tried to look useful. Fiscally viable.

Then he turned back. A broad grin stretching across the man's face.

And Matt's heart dropped.

He was laughing. "I's sorry," he said, "I couldn't keep a straight face." Then the gun went up. "Get up. On youse feet."

Matt did as he was instructed, being careful with his damaged leg.

The man came, the gun trained on him at all times. He dropped the clasp from his wrist.

"Are you letting me go?" he whispered. Hope leaping into his chest, filling his heart. Brief, wild, hope.

"Yeah," he said. "Le'ing you go."

Then dashed. The way he said it. It was a lie. *Of course,* it was a lie. They weren't going to let him go.

Moving him to *the machine*, perhaps. That again. The man moved around behind him and jabbed the gun in Matt's back. He tried to support himself, nearly falling to the ground, his legs barely under him.

"There, there," the man said. "Youse just weak."

Maybe they *were* letting him go?

"Come on." The man jabbed Matt in the back again and pushed him forward.

Matt stumbled, desperately trying to stay on his feet. Rubbing his wrist, now free. The skin is bruised and purple. Scuffed. Dried blood surrounds it. He was naked. So cold. He felt his bowels turn. Little in there, he wasn't going to shit. Just the motion of walking. It felt like he'd been chained up in there for so, so long. Stomach then turned. Hungry. A warmth danced over his flesh, feeling the sunlight hit it as he left whatever shade the barn was giving him. The cool breeze on his skin, raising goosebumps on his flesh, raw and hard.

"Don't youse get too excited," the man said. "This way." He pushed him again, leading him to the right. Towards some of the pens. Certainly not freedom. He swallowed hard. Throat arid. The dirt outside was hard on his feet, dry, dusty, but warmer than that fucking barn they'd been holding him.

"Stop."

Matt did as he was told. He was wavering slightly, trying to stay on his feet. Hard to tell up from down in the barn all the time, but his head now, standing in fresh air, the sun … so lightheaded. Waves of dizziness washing over him. He watched the man go around him from behind, the gun on him the whole time. To a fenced-in area. He drew the bolt across opening it. The metal clanged and the gate opened. The long, drawn creak of it being pulled back while he watched.

Most certainly not … *freedom*.

Daisy watched as the master went to the building on the right. He looked angry. It was bad that the master was angry, but also good. That usually meant that lunch was going to be good. She turned and looked at her brother. He was watching, too. They both knew what it meant.

She was waiting, in anticipation. There were sounds in the building. Then they came. The naked man in front. Yes. Raw. Uncut. They were coming straight to them. Fresh to the farmer's table—as it were. Daisy watched the master open the pen. She scurried to the side, her brother pushing against her.

The meat spoke some foreign tongue. Didn't matter. The master hit him from behind. Then he stumbled forward.

Daisy lurched at the meat. Didn't even notice the gate being closed behind it. Didn't care. She opened her mouth and clamped down on the meat's leg. Teeth broken and sharp, digging into the flesh. The meat screamed out in surprise at the pain and dropped to the ground. She closed her jaw tightly, feeling the bones in the meat break, shattering under the force. Blood, warm and sticky, letting into her mouth, tasty. She swallowed the blood back and she tore at it, pulling the flesh and bone back, as the meat screamed and flailed. Her brother chowed into the meat's shoulder, teeth deep, blood spewing up his face as he yanked the ball of bone free from within the flesh.

She pulled the leg, dragging it back to the edge of the pen, the bones crunching in her mouth as she ground them to rice. The warmth of fresh flesh, bitter, sticking to the roof of her mouth.

The calm of the farm was broken by the screams of the meat as her brother retreated with his mouth full.

The flesh wouldn't move for long. He was haemorrhaging blood. Bits of bone drop from the wounds. Daisy stopped and looked at her prize, the leg. Then back to the squirming feast, still fresh and warm. Back to the leg. She trampled it, leaving it for later, going back to the buffet for more. The meat was still blinded and bound. Rolling in the decaying filth and blood blackened mud. It's back to her now, she dug in, tearing his fingers from his hand, swallowing them whole. Her brother came to the front of it—taking her lead—tearing his fat cock from his body, chewing his balls. He shuddered, stopping the flail and flopping flat. Blood pumping from his wounds, still alive. But unconscious. She stepped up on it, rolling it onto it's back. Looking down onto the flesh, the belly, flat and round, bloated from gas. She tore into it, ripping it open, the smell of meat stink coming out. She swallowed back the boneless tenderloin, her brother nosed his way into the wound, looking for the intestines, guts, and offal.

Daisy dropped down. Rounded her brother, his

face a mess of gore and blood from the meat, and to the head of it. She looked into its face. Gurned into some horror show of fear and pain. Then she leant forward, her teeth sinking into it's face, the skull cracking under the force, skin tearing away, as she chewed the meat's flesh from the head. Spitting it out to the muck below, snout snuffling around the smell of human brain. A sweet and sickly stink that cut through the metal of the blood. She pushed into the remnant of the skull, a bowl offering warm brain and fleshy goo, mixing into a soup, perfect and succulent. Her tongue lapping it into her mouth, and when she was sated, she rounded her pig-bother still eating the flesh from the torso and looked at the master who watched. Looking for some sign of happiness.

He nodded, and grinned. Happy with her performance.

And that made Daisy happy, too.

She loved the master with all her heart.

C H A P T E R   2

Reggie opened her mouth and pushed the bacon in. It was flabby. Undercooked in her opinion. She'd never been skiing but was pretty sure that the breakfast at what she assumed would be a lodge, would be better than this. Unless it was Alpen. She could have had that here if she'd chosen the continental breakfast. She looked at Richard. He was smiling into his coffee.

Cock.

She smiled at him. Tried to bring some warmth to it. "So what's the plan today?" she asked. "More walking?"

He grunted. Probably not really listening.

"Or more driving?"

Richard had decided that they hadn't seen enough of the country that they lived in. So, it was what he called a 'driving holiday.' Staying at random places in the middle of random nowhere, eating random bacon. She looked at the next piece of bacon on her fork. It wasn't even smoked.

"Yes," he said. "I like it around here."

That was when she was sure he wasn't listening at all, and quite possibly having a completely different conversation with her in his head. She watched him attack his egg white, flailing to turn it over and over and fork the fucking thing. "It's too rubbery for that."

He stopped and looked at her. A sly grin. "That's what she said." Then he pushed it in his mouth.

That didn't even make sense. She shook herself from her thoughts and tried the sausage again. Maybe this bite would taste better. Then she ignored the look from Richard and gazed around the restaurant attached to the hotel. If you could call it a hotel. It was one of those places that catered for business people that have shot up everywhere, because they're cheap. And that was it, wasn't it? They were doing this because it was cheap—or cheaper—than going skiing. Like she'd wanted. She watched the old man on the table over the way pour the jug of water into his wife's glass. They looked about eighty. This was probably their annual holiday too. That was what they were becoming, wasn't it? Eighty-year-olds staying in cheap hotels with shit breakfasts. Christ and strike a light they were old people. She swallowed the meat. And listen to her. *Strike a light?* That was something her old man used to say when she was a kid. She *was* turning into an old person. Right there, at the table. She was turning into her parents, doing what her parents do. Did. Whatever. She wasn't even forty yet and she was *thinking* like an old aged pensioner. "Cunt," she blurted.

Richard cleared his throat, calling her attention back.

She hadn't meant to linger at the nice old man when she'd taken it upon herself to explete in a young person's way. Fuck. Do kids even say cunt anymore? It's probably something else. Something … rappy. She smiled at Richard and said, "Yo," and then carried on eating. At least she could see the funny side of that. She glanced at the old man. He'd paid her no mind, but that might have been because his hearing aids were probably turned off. She looked over, to the table with the younger people on. They were only what … twenty? Something like that. They were having the continental breakfast. It was a little cheaper. Probably because you don't get any meat. She liked the meat. That was another thing. Her attention was back to Richard. "All this country air," she said. "Why aren't you screwing my brains out every night?" She raised her eyebrows, expectantly.

Richard started to choke. Taking a sip of his water and looking around apologetically in case anyone heard. "Whatever do you mean?" he hissed.

She put her fork down and raised a finger. "We are in the countryside and not in a skiing lodge. I want to know why you haven't been entertaining me nightly with your sexual prowess."

Richard looked around again. This time, perhaps, because of what she'd said about his prowess. "I've been driving. I'm tired."

She picked her fork back up. "So, I go without …" She speared the remnant of her sausage, lifting it, "… my sausage," she finished.

Richard was wide-eyed. He sighed. "I will see to

you when we get back to the room."

Better had do, she thought. She stuffed the sausage in her mouth and chewed loudly. He was very good in the sack, actually. Something about shy men and people who were withdrawn. Introverted. He'd taken the time to learn to do what she wanted. Knew how to please her and wasn't bothered about himself so much. She smiled and picked up her toast. "Well hurry up then. I want mine."

He snorted a laugh.

———

"Fuck," she whispered. Richard was tongue deep inside her. "Fuck me," she said. He stroked her g-spot with his tip and then slipped it out, circling her clit. The orgasm was ready to fire wildly through her. "Jesus Christ." She was keeping her voice down—she'd heard next door's TV a little while ago and didn't need the whole hotel knowing that her husband could draw orgasms from her with his mouth in seconds. Her fingers wrapped around the sheet, pulled into a fist as she bloomed. Her mouth squeezed shut, the squeal held within. She pushed her legs closed, forcing Richard out, stopping him from teasing her to a second. She couldn't take that again. "Fuck," she whispered, again.

Richard crawled up the bed and held her, pulling the covers over. Her juices slicked around his mouth and face.

The two of them laying there for long moments.

Reggie opened her eyes. He was gone. She blinked

and looked at the clock. Fuck me. It was nearly eleven. She sat, looking around the room. Blinking. Holding the warm covers over herself. Jesus. "Babe?"

The toilet flushed.

She drew air in, and quickly slipped from the bed, pulling her clothes on before he came out the toilet. By the time he did, she was in jeans and t-shirt.

"Did I wake you?"

She shook her head. "Lunch," she asked, grinning.

He laughed. "I just ate."

Reggie picked up the pillow from the bed and tossed it at him, him batting it away. "Right–I think we should hit the village and see what the town has to offer."

"The village?" she asked, a sigh escaping her lips.

"Lower Crumbsbottom," he said.

Lower … whatever. Great. Village? It was going to be a quaint pub full of weirdos, a church that was looking for donations for a new roof and a Premier shop with a post office inside that wanted sixty pence for a Freddo. Fuckers. She sighed, again. Best get the displeasure out of the way. They'd had a barney in the car yesterday before they'd gotten to this place.

She grabbed up her coat. "Come on then. But I want lunch and a glass of wine."

The two of them left the room and went down to the car.

"So, where is this village?" she asked, getting in

the passenger seat.

Richard tapped his phone screen, slipping in next to her. "GPS," he replied.

Clearly no idea, then. Great. "Where'd you find it?"

"Poking around on the map." He stuffed his phone in the little pouch he had that hung off the vent by the door—something Reggie had gotten him for Christmas one year. He started the engine and took them off to the road. The GPS recalibrating before telling him to turn … *right*.

———

Reggie looked quickly to the car, parked at the side of the road, on the outskirts of this village that Richard had found on his phone the night before. She was sure he'd locked it and was about to lose sight of it. She stepped to the corner of the stone bridge over the babbling brook, and leant against it, watching Richard trying to get lower down the bank without getting his feet wet to take a photo. She was smiling like he was already pointing the camera at her.

She was just being silly. It was sweet, wasn't it?

Wasn't it?

Her eyes drifted from him to the buildings further up the bank. *Lower Crumbsbottom*. What kind of name is that for a village? She was sure he would find someone to ask if he could. She returned her eyes to him, in time for him to twist his ankle and spin out. It looked funny. Almost in slow motion. Like he was about to do a cartwheel. Except he wasn't. He was screaming. And then he was wet. In the brook.

Reggie let her head drop. "Right," she muttered to herself, pushing herself from the stones and heading down to him. He was on his hands and knees in the water. It was maybe a foot deep. Arsehat. He was staring at her. Had the look of a frightened child. She got to the side of the bank and stepped into the shallow bit. Held her hand out. "Hand?" she said.

He didn't move.

"What? Are you hurt?" She didn't need that. Take him to the hospital? Have to do the rest of the driving on the driving holiday? Ugh.

He lifted his left hand from the water. The phone. He had it out to take a photo. "I'm sorry," he said.

She shook her head. "It'll be fine. Hand." She waved him towards her, and he got to his knees, taking her hand. The two of them managed to get him to the bank. He looked down at himself. "Shit."

"You're wet," she said, taking the phone. She looked at it. Pressed the button to switch it on. "Fucked," she said, sighing.

He took it back, almost snatching it. His little baby. "It'll be fine once it dries out."

"I'm sure," she said. "Pint?" She looked back towards the buildings. "I think I saw a pub back there. Probably do all sorts of real ales."

"Hm," he said, half nodding, half agreeing, half

not paying attention to her.. He started walking—hobbling—back to the car, and she followed. He put the phone screen-side down on the dash in the sun. Then turned to her. "Glass of wine?"

She knew he hadn't been listening. "That's a good idea. Think there's a pub?"

He nodded, leading the way. "I think I saw one on the way in."

"Did you? Oh." She shook her head smiling as she followed. Slowly.

Into the mouth of the village they went, hand in hand, mostly because she was struggling to keep pace with him now that he was lame. The houses were old, stone, and flint affairs. Things painted white years ago and now the paint flaking away. The road was without a path and tarmac, grass verged without drainage. It was like the twentieth century hadn't happened.

"There's a village pub," Richard said, dropping her hand away, pointing.

"I think they'll probably just call it, *the pub*," she said.

"What's that?"

He wasn't listening again. "Never mind." Reggie reached in and grabbed his hand back. She looked down at his trousers. Wet. "Maybe they'll dry out in there," she whispered.

He wasn't listening.

——

"Swimming you say?"

Richard laughed. "Yes. I … a little." He looked down at his wet trouser legs. He couldn't tell when he looked like he was flirting because he was silly. He picked up the pint and the wine and returned to the table. "They have a dry white. Opened a new bottle," he said, putting the wine down.

"Good." Reggie smiled, immediately taking the glass and tasting it. Not exactly the quality of wine one would get in the lodge, but it would suffice. She watched him over the rim of her glass, sipping his. "Good?" she asked.

He nodded, his voice dropping to a whisper. "They only have commercial stuff. Apparently, they've run out of the cask stuff."

Reggie nodded along with the words. "I see." So, not good then? She shrugged and enjoyed the wine, regardless. "What else do they have here?"

"There's a High Street."

Fucking hell. It's a miracle. Actual shops. "We'll check that out, yes? How's your ankle?"

"It's fine. Feeling much better."

Of course it was. A chat with the hot barmaid and a pint of beer. It was all forgotten. She blinked too much and continued with the wine. "Hungry?" she asked.

"They only have salt and vinegar."

Crisps. The be-all and end-all of pub food. "No thank you. Chippie?"

"I'll ask." He pushed himself from the table and she watched him return to the barmaid. Blond. Pretty. Big tits. Small shirt. She toyed with her hair while verbally playing with Reggie's husband. Silly, innocent boy, Reggie thought, smiling to herself. They exchanged a few words and then he returned to the chair. "No."

"Right. So, what do we do for food?"

"There's a supermarket on the edge of the village just before the A249. Apparently, that's the best place."

Reggie nodded. Right. Supermarket food. "Nice," she said. "Supermarket food." She shook her head, getting up from the chair herself and going to the bar. The big titty blonde tart was making pouty faces into her phone. Reggie leaned on the bar. "Anything to do around here?" she asked—except other people's husbands (internal snort).

The woman flicked her eyes up from the screen and stared at her for a second, as if the worlds slowest cogs turned. "There are some scenic walks," she said.

"Picnic spots?" Reggie asked.

She shrugged. "You can always stop in a field. Farmers don't mind as long as you don't nick nothing."

"I best not nick nothing now," Reggie said, grinning. "Any shops on the High Street?"

"Mr. Downes has a shop that sells all sorts."

"Liquorice?"

The woman looked dumbfounded.

"Never mind. Thank you." Reggie returned to the seats, Richard staring out to the street beyond the window. "So, we walk up to High Street, and look at the liquorice in Downes place, and then eat in the supermarket. Maybe go for a walk. Lots of walks apparently."

"You don't like it here much, do you?" he asked, without taking his look from the world outside.

"It's growing on me."

C H A P T E R   3

"I told you we should have bought some rice." Richard jabbed the phone with his thumb. "It's still wet."

"Uh-huh." Reggie wasn't really listening. She was staring in the mirror in the bathroom, applying her eyeliner. Regardless of what Richard said, going on a walk and having a picnic, she had appearances to keep up. She turned out of the bathroom and looked at the carrier bag with their picnic, sitting on the dresser-turned-desk that all cheap hotels had. Richard was sitting in the single 'cuck' chair they all had, too. The one that faces the bed, that no one, apart from Richard, ever found a reason to sit in.

She picked up the bag containing picnic food from the supermarket . Supermarket was a grandiose term in all fairness. It was a shitty little place that overcharged. But when weren't they? On this all-encompassing driving holiday. She sighed and looked at Richard, jabbing at the screen. Skiing. Could have been skiing. "Coming then?" she said, turning out of the bathroom.

Richard put the phone on the cuck table and followed her out. "We need to get some rice from somewhere."

"What?" she muttered, following in the corridor around to the stairs.

"To dry out the phone. I read it online."

"And you think that's going to work, do you?"

"Apparently." He held the door open for her and the two of them went to the car. Carrier in the boot.

Then, as they sat there, in the car, unstarted, she said, "What are we waiting for?"

"I don't know where I'm going." He looked at her. "The GPS is the phone, isn't it?"

Reggie rubbed her forehead, irritated. "Great."

"Look," he continued. "I'll just run us back to the village from yesterday, and instead of going into the High street, we'll just wander off into the fields."

"How will you know what's a footpath and what's not?"

He started the engine. "Nice girl at the pub said the farmers wouldn't mind, didn't she?"

Nice girl at the pub.

"So, does it matter? Besides, there's sure to be signs up." He flashed her a smile. "Besides. It'll be an adventure."

She nodded. An adventure.

———

"An adventure," she said. He was stumbling over the stile between the fields. Richard was standing, his back to her, as he gazed out over the turned fields. Hand over his eyes, shielding them from the sun.

She got down and went to his side. "Which way Captain?" She made sure to slap the piss on the words thick enough that even he wouldn't miss it. Yet he did.

He pointed. "That-a way." Then he took the carrier bag of food and started to yomp again.

Reggie sighed and followed. Sure. She was happy to do the walking thing. To some extent, the driving thing. Hell, it *was* a holiday. Albeit a strange one that didn't include skis. She shook her head, yelping quietly under her breath as her ankle turned a funny direction … again.

"Let's stop at that copse of trees for a break," he said, pointing forward

"Copse," she muttered back. "Sure." She could feel the tightness of her breathing. She'd had a bad flu over the winter previous, and while she was sure she should be better by now, she wasn't fully healed. The sun was warm, but there in the fields, there was a fresh breeze that ran over everything. Chilling you to the bone.

As they crossed, Richard sunk down into the grass verging with the field in the shade. He pulled a can of off-brand cola from the carrier and popped it open. Reggie stood over him. Looking down. In the shade. She was going to catch another chill if she wasn't careful. But she shook it away. This was his holiday, too. She sat down with him and took the can when he offered it forward, slurping some of the saccharin sweetness from the can.

"What do you think about tomorrow?" he asked.

"What about it?"

"Want to hit the road early?"

She looked out to the field. There was something peaceful out there. The gentle wind—even if it was cold—, the clear blue of the sky. A quietness laying over everything, a little like a horror movie. She smiled to herself. It was, dare she admit it, nice. She shook her head. "No," she replied. "I want to stay here for another day. Let's do a proper picnic tomorrow. Let's find a trail and walk it and picnic. Like this is a proper holiday."

"Proper holiday," he echoed, grinning widely at her, happy that she'd finally taken the plunge and accepted this is the *only* holiday. "Good," he said, mimicking some voice from an old movie.

They continued to sit there for a while. Long minutes as they absorbed the peace. The tranquil. The sound of some machinery in some field far away. A tractor in the other direction. "I don't hear a lot of birds," she finally said.

Richard shook his head, appearing to only be half listening. "Maybe they're doing what the seagulls at home do, and they are trailing that tractor."

"Nah."

The voice from behind them made them both turn hurriedly. "Jesus," snapped Richard.

"Oh, noes," the woman said, standing over the

hedge behind them. "It's just me, Maisie." Then she started to laugh as if the words were some sort of joke. She was a plump woman, you could tell, even as she hung over the hedgerow behind them. Her face slightly too red, like she'd been out in the sun too long, although too much alcohol could also do that to you, Reggie knew. She was wearing a body warmer over a chequered shirt. Probably about forty. Maybe a little older. "So, what are you twose doing down 'ere?"

Richard glanced around. His first thought was that they'd strayed too far and were in trouble on someone's private property. "I'm sorry," he said. "We were just walking."

"Oh, you hush," she said. "There ain't nut'in' wrong with you walking 'bout these fields, mind you don't get prodded by no bull." She put her hands to her head and mimicked a bull's horns, fingers out. Then started laughing again. "I's only jesting. No. You just need to watch out for the tractors. Timothy sometimes gets caught up in his music—if youse can call it that, payin' no mind to which way he's going." More laughing.

"Oh, we will," said Reggie, smiling, just trying to work out what this woman was getting at.

She flickered her look from Richard to Reggie, and then back again. Rude. Then continued, "So wha', you on holiday, love?"

Richard nodded, pushing himself to his feet, hand extended, and the two of them shook, over the hedge, her pushing herself up to reach over. "Why, yes. We were just taking in the scenery. We are all right to be out here, then?" He put on his slightly posher voice.

Reggie wondered if the woman might take offence, what with her sounding so ... farmer ... about it all.

"Oh, youse all right. Me and my 'usband own all this, far as the eye can see. So, you don't worry about nut'in'. Try not to get lost, though." Again, laughter. "But if youse do, you follow the hills to the side, and you'll come to the farmhouse eventually. We can always drive you back into town. You staying at that fancy 'otel?"

Richard nodded. Fancy. Yes.

"My sister-in-law works there at the weekends. Says she gets a lot of visitors from London. Youse from London?"

"No," Richard answered. He glanced at Reggie, still sitting, his eyes pleading with her for rescue. Which was not forthcoming. "We're from down south on the coast."

"Oh, nice. I do like to be beside the seaside." She grinned. "So look. I'll leave you two to it. If you want to return tomorrow, you see anybody, you tell 'em Maisie said it was okay." She nodded like a Churchill dog. "That's *Maisie*," she said. Hand out for another shake, which Richard obliged. She eyed him. Something there in the look, Reggie saw. Then she was gone, back behind the bush.

Reggie stifled a laugh, covering her mouth, as Richard returned to sit and took the coke. "I think she liked you," she said.

"Oh yes," he replied, faking up a northern accent. "I've got the bundiest chompers in the clundy."

Reggie shook her head. "But she seemed nice. Maybe we could come back this way tomorrow with a proper picnic."

"That's a lovely idea. We can leave the car in the same place and go that way." He pointed out to the far side of the field, the trees over to the left of where they sat, out to a different field.

"Have to watch out for Tim and his tractor and his tunes."

C H A P T E R   4

The next morning, Richard and Reggie left earlier. They headed to the supermarket again. The car, parked in the small car park outside the small supermarket, Richard leaned against the side of it while Reggie sorted out the bags in the boot. She wanted to sort the picnic out. Even bought a blanket in the shitty place. Richard looked up the side of the building. It looked about a thousand years old. Then to Reggie's arse, sticking out the boot. Yes, a blanket, along with what looked like substandard pork pies.

You'd have thought that pork pies from up north would be better than pork pies from down south, what with the Melton Mowbray connection and all, but these looked somewhat ropey. He smiled to himself and shook his head. He didn't know what to do without his phone, but at least they bought some rice. Get the phone in that tonight and hope it was enough. The problem with having all these fixes online was that you could never remember them when you needed them. He snorted to himself.

Reggie slammed the boot—too hard—and came around to him. "It's all packed," she said. "Let's go." Richard leant in and kissed her on the neck. She squeaked, and the two of them got into the car, pulling out, and returning the way they came to the village.

Crumbsbottom.

———

Reggie handed the picnic basket over—which they didn't really need, but she'd insisted, because it was proper—to Richard, to carry. He took it without a word and took her hand in his. He led them, but without dragging, as they just ambled together in the warm sun.

They crossed from the edge of the village to the field on the side—near the brook—and climbed the first fence.

Making their way down into the field, they started to follow the treeline. The wind whistled up the hill and Reggie shivered, pulling her arms around herself. "Jeepers," she said.

"Jinkies," he returned.

"Fucker," she said.

He laughed. "You want my jacket?"

She shook her head, pushing herself closer into his body. "Nah. You're all right." They kept a little out of the shade of the trees, for which she was glad. "So where to next?" she asked, finally.

"I'd have thought you were ready for home." Richard looked down at her, her shoulder forced under his arm.

"I'm getting the hang of this. So, we drive for too

long. Fuck in a hotel room for a couple of days. Fall in something. And eat." She grinned up at him.

"Sounds about right," he said, quietly. Mulling the summation of their holiday around in his head, driving, food, and fucking. Could have been worse.

"Fine. So," she asked, looking around, "when are we going to fuck on a blanket in the middle of a field?" She laughed.

"Perhaps when Mrs. Pork Pie, the farmer's wife, might not be watching from a bush somewhere." His laugh joined hers. "How about here?" he asked, pointing to a large tree in the corner of the field.

"Sounds good." She took the bag with the blanket and unfolded it to lay on the grass. The two of them sat, half in the shade and half out of it, away from the tractor tire marks. Eating slightly shit pork pies.

Reggie squinted to the far side of the field. "Look," she said. Over there, there were two figures.

Richard made some sort of acknowledgement and looked over his pie at them. He wiped his mouth with a serviette. It was a man and a woman. The man was carrying something. Richard chewed silently while Reggie looked from them to him. "What do you think?" she asked.

Richard shrugged. "Not a clue. Probably some farm hands. What was her name? Maisie? We just have to tell them that Maisie said it was okay for us to be here."

"What if this isn't her family's field?"

Richard looked at her. "Then we'll apologise and be on our way. It's not like we're sitting in the corner of the field shoving lambs into our bags, is it?" He squinted at them again. "Besides," he said finally. "It is Maisie." Pointing and then waving. He glanced to Reggie. "See, everything's all right."

Reggie nodded, slow. She raised her hand in a half wave too, then pushed the remains of her pork pie in the bag, chewing quickly to clear her mouth.

"'Ello there," Maisie called from too far away.

Richard didn't want to shout, so he waited for them to be closer. And as they got closer, he realised that the other person—a man—was carrying a gun. He glanced at Reggie. She'd noticed the same thing. "It's okay," he hissed quietly enough that the approaching couple wouldn't be able to hear. "They're farmers. It's for game or something."

Game or something … yes. Reggie returned her look to them and smiled as broadly as she could. She'd never seen a gun before. Not in real life. He had it open and hanging over his arm. The two of them, closer now she could see, were close to the same age. Perhaps, *Mr.* Maisie.

"So," Maisie said, now close enough not to be shouting. "This 'ere is my 'usband. Lewis."

"Lewis," said Richard. He started to push himself to stand, to introduce himself properly and shake the man's hand, but Lewis waved for him to sit. Then he looked at Reggie. Saw her watching his gun. "It's okay, Ma'am. Totally 'armless when she's open like this. Can't hurt a fly."

Reggie nodded, clearly nervous.

"''Ow you twose doin' then? Out for 'nother picnic?"

"Yes," Richard said. Posh voice again. "It's quite delightful around these parts."

Reggie just wanted to have the ground swallow her up. If these two got a whiff that he was putting on a voice, they might take it the wrong way and think he was taking the piss. Which he wasn't. It was just his 'company' voice. Her eyes dropped to the gun again. And they have a gun. She swallowed, suddenly dry. "So, what are you hunting?" she said, far too quickly and without thought. Cutting into the proceedings.

Lewis raised the gun a little. "She's 'unting trespassers." Reggie drew air in, and he laughed. "Oh noes. Don't you worry lit'le lady. Rabbits. Wascally things." The laughter rose from the two of them and Reggie looked on, nervous. She bumped her way a little closer to Richard.

"It's fine," he whispered.

"So," continued Lewis. "These the two you bumped into on the field yesterday?"

Maisie nodded. "Yes, this is them."

"'Im?" he said.

Richard raised his eyebrows. "Me?"

"Youse," said Maisie.

"Right-o." Lewis quickly removed the shotgun

from his arm and snapped it closed. The sound of it cutting through Reggie. "I'll make this painless," he continued. Lewis raised the gun up and waved it in the direction of Reggie.

She screamed, turning into a spin and trying to roll away.

Then the air filled with the sound of the gunshot.

Shotgun. Up close. It sounded like a jet engine starting up. Birds flew from the trees. The echo bounced around the field. Richard sat there. Staring. Blinking. Shock gripped him. He couldn't move. He had warm, sticky blood on his face. Eyes growing wider. This tinnitus sound filling his ears. *Eeeeeeeeeeeeeeeeeeee.*

Reggie rolled onto her back. The same sound filled her head. A whistle she couldn't shake. She turned her head, now on her back, and looked at Richard. He was sitting as he had been. She felt … numb. Cocked her arm up underneath her. Looked at the blood. There was blood everywhere.

Then the scream of pain started. Crawling from her leg. Up her body like the sear of a red-hot poker stuffed violently under the skin. She looked to Maisie. She was laughing like this was all some big joke. Lewis. He was shaking his head. Looked pissed. He was saying something she couldn't hear. The whistling stopped her from hearing anything apart from her own melodic breathing.

She could taste blood. It was in her mouth.

Then she looked at down herself. Her leg was

gone. Well—technically, it was still there, but it wasn't attached, per se, anymore. The new blanket was covered in her blood.

She looked at Richard. He was still staring at them. Paying her no mind. She said his name to get his attention, but she didn't hear her own voice. He couldn't either, clearly. The pain was rising. It wasn't manageable. That feeling that was rising up, over her gut, the burn. That was what made her scream. Cry.

Richard was shaking. He could feel himself shaking. Like he'd been in a car crash and he was just sitting there, holding the steering wheel, waiting for the world to stop going around. The cold crept in. Maybe that was why he shook? He looked to the left. The sound of the world taken by the shot. Looked at Reggie. She was covered in blood. Her blood. He looked down at himself. Not his. He wasn't bleeding. He had to do something. This fucking maniac's gun had misfired. Gone off. They needed to call an ambulance. Fucking hell. They needed a lawyer. He moved his hands around under him and pushed. Wobbling. Hard. *It was the shock*, he was telling himself, but he had to help Reggie. *Get the leg on ice*, he thought, staring at it as he heaved himself to his feet. He stood there for a second. No more. Looking at the leg. The blood not circulating his body quite right. He felt … sick. Can't puke on the leg. Need to keep it safe. He looked at the farmers. He needed their help. He thought he said something. Then the man … *what was his name. Lewis? Yes*. He stepped forward and raised the gun. A look of hate and anger in his features. Looked like he was going to—

The butt of the shotgun landed on Richard's nose and his brain shook as he stumbled back and fell. Over something. The last thought in his head, that of the leg.

Reggie watched him drop, stumbling back and tripping partly over the picnic hamper and partly over her leg. The one that was still attached. She was screaming a silent scream. One that eluded her ears. Her useless, whining ears. Eyes on Lewis. The pain ravaging her. She turned. Her stump flailing about as her body willed parts of her no longer attached to move. He was going to kill them. He'd attacked Richard now. It was on purpose. They were going to kill them.

She clawed at the soil beyond the blanket and pulled, dragging herself on her belly. Blood pumping from her harder as she fought to flee. Her eyes on Richard, his face bleeding, seeping into the dirt next to her. Then she stopped. The pain was too much, and she wasn't getting anywhere. She turned and looked at Lewis and Maisie. He had his gun up. Again, pointing at her. He was laughing now, the two of them a chorus. She could even begin to hear them as the incessant whistle began to die down.

He pointed the gun, and he fired it.

The whistle returned in force. Her body went numb. The pain from her leg, gone suddenly. She cried out. Thought she did, anyway. Rolled onto her back and looked. Her other leg was a mess. The shot this time, not ripping through her completely, but rather leaving a mess of blood and bone. She could feel a sickness in her stomach. Rancid and burning. Her legs were gone. They were broken and torn. She wasn't ever going to walk again. She looked up at him. He had the gun open. Pulling the empties from it and tossing them to the side.

Reggie looked around the field. Someone must have heard. Someone must have. Surely. She could feel the wet tears on her face. The world spinning slightly slower. She was so cold. She lay back. Tired. Wanted to stop and rest. Just for a moment.

Then Lewis stood over her. He was chewing something. Looking down on her, gun up. It was pointed at her below her face. To her torso. He was going to fire again. This was the last thing she was going to see, wasn't it? She turned her head. Looked at Richard.

C H A P T E R   5

"Get the fuck off me." Timothy shook Anton's hand from his shoulder. Anton laughed. Grating laugh he had. Silly. Sounded like a fucking duck … fucking. "Bitch," he said.

"Bitch," Anton replied. He let his hand drop, and he went and retrieved another bowl from the cabinet. Brought it to the breakfast bar and poured some wheaty flakes into it. Topped it down with milk. He sat on the stool and spooned a large mouthful. Chewed thoughtfully for a second and then said, "So, what's the plan for today?"

Tim shrugged. "I don't know. Uni work I suppose."

"Sounds fun." Anton snorted.

"You?" Tim was shovelling toast into his mouth like his life depended on it.

"I might go for a walk. Get some fresh air."

"Spent too much time in the old smoke recently?"

"Deffo."

The two of them giggled like schoolchildren,

mostly at their faux proper accents. Tim pushed himself to stand. Lifted his mug and raised it to Anton. "Another?"

"Please."

Tim rounded the floating island and went to the side and started to prepare a couple more mugs of coffee. He stared at the yard outside the window. A walk wasn't a bad idea, but he had to get some of this fucking work done. He'd be due back on campus before he knew it and he'd barely started. He glanced over at Anton. Lucky bastard had foregone the rigours of university and gone straight to work. Perhaps he should have done that, instead of trying to better himself. Make a new life. A different one to the rest of the family. Apart from Jean. Jean was his sister. She'd escaped this life. He shook his head, thinking about her.

"What's the matter?" Anton said, rounding the side and standing next to him.

"Just thinking about Jean."

"She'll be home soon. You'll see her then." Anton raised his arm and put it over Tim's shoulders, pulling him in closer. "You'll see."

The two of them looked out the window for a moment, together. There was a light wind, enough to move the trees in the distance. Tim reached around behind Anton and rested his hand on his arse. A little squeeze. "Have you seen mother this morning?" Anton flinched under his touch. Then he pulled away.

"No, why?"

"I just wondered. I think she's been absent recently."

"Well, you know her and father have been trying for another child, don't you?"

Tim looked back at his brother, retreating with his coffee back to the breakfast bar. "Really?"

"Well, you do spend time away from the family." Anton's smile was fake. He looked smug and angry all at the same time.

"Isn't she getting a little … past it?" Tim snorted a laugh, then swallowed it away. That was the sort of talk that got you whipped by Father. "So, she wants another little one?" He shook his head. "I'm not really surprised." He spoke with an air of education. "You know how broody these women get once the kids start to fly the nest. Jean first. Me." He looked down at his brother. "So, when are you going to do something … useful?"

Anton squinted at him. "I'm doing just fine, you know."

"Fine? Doing what Father says more like."

"You'll be sorry when I'm running this place—"

"And I have a house in the Docklands."

"Where?" Anton sneered.

"Canary wharf, perhaps."

"Sounds darling," Anton replied, pretending to know nothing of the city. Belittle it. Make his brother angry. "I have everything I need here."

Tim stood to Anton's side. He rested his hand down on top of his brothers. "Not everything," he whispered.

Anton looked at the top of his brother's hand before slipping his from underneath. He felt the ice in Tim's touch. There was something spiteful there, even when he didn't mean it. "Enough," he said quietly. "What would Mother say?"

Tim snorted. Always with the same excuses. "Quite a lot." He pulled his mobile from his pocket and looked at the time. "Are we supposed to be doing lunch today?"

"I think so," Anton spoke quietly. His mind elsewhere in thought.

"Fine." Tim pushed himself to stand. "Probably shouldn't have slept in so late, then."

———

Lewis pulled the clothing from Richard roughly, watching him carefully, ensuring he didn't wake. Not while he wasn't paying attention. You could get a fist in the face for that. He yanked his trousers down and pulled his pants with them. Looked at his flaccid little penis. Shook his head. Hopefully, it would grow. He smiled. Maisie gets what Maisie wants.

He clamped the metal clasp around his wrist and tested the weight of the chain on the wall. Made sure he was secure. That would do for now. Until they knew how they had to play this.

He turned and left the barn. A glance over at the cows. The calves were only days old. Already up and walking and doing their taxes. Made you wonder why human children were so fucking slow for the majority of their formative years. He stopped at the barn door, looking back at Richard.

"Dick," he said to himself. A quiet smile. Then he closed the door and headed for the tractor. He hopped up into the cab and started her up to a purr. "Oh, yes," he said, patting her on the steering wheel. He pulled her backwards, and then around, to the gates at the back of the property line and into the fields. Heading back the way he'd come.

Driving between the fields of yellow, rapeseed on one side, hay on the other. Along the hedgerows, until he could see the field where they left the dead girl. He pulled up, other side of the hedge to the corpse. Lewis climbed over the wall and came around. Looked down on the girl. The shotgun had all but ripped her in half. He looked at his watch … over and hour ago. She'd be getting cold by now. He hunched over the body and started to pull her clothes off. He'd stop at the field at the back of thc Farmhouse where the composter was and drop them off there. Covered in blood and bits of woman, but that was fine. Most of it went to pig feed, anyway. He was careful not to break her in half, pulling the ragged material from her. Easier to get in the back of the tractor is she was still in one piece …

Lewis looked down on her naked body. Breathing through his nose. Yes. He took the clothes back over the wall and tossed them in the back of the tractor, stepped up on the wheel at the back and looked back, and around the fields.

Nothing but birds.

He then stepped down and went to the girl. Sticky. Naked. Gaping hole in her.

Yes.

C H A P T E R   6

Cold. That was the first thing he felt. Then the pain. Aches. Everything, all at once. Richard turned on the … ground. He was *on* the ground. Why? Where the fuck was he? He lay there for a moment, letting the memories return. Waiting. Fuck. He opened his eyes and looked at the ceiling above him. The beams crawling across the darkness. A smell. Something below the smell of blood. He could smell *blood*.

Reggie.

He looked to the side. Moved his head. The pain cranked around inside him like he was on fire. "Fuck," he muttered. He waited for the world to stop turning. Again. He blinked it away. "Reggie, honey?" He breathed through his mouth. Nose hurt. Face hurt. He remembered … those farmers. Then noise. He was … fuck. *Reggie*. She was hurt. He rolled to the side, suddenly his hand snapped back, stopping him. The rattle of chains. He could hear again. That was something. He rolled back the other way. Looked at the chain holding him to the panel, bolted to the wall. Confused, he looked around. "Hello?" he called. A sudden rise in noise as animals moved and made weird alien sounds.

What the hell was going on?

He slumped back to the floor for a moment. Tried to get his bearings. He was … where? He looked around, squinting in the half-light of the closed-up building. There were shards of light creeping in through gaps in the wooden walls, sunlight coming in from outside. He focused on the things around him. Stalls for animals—pens. There were machines in the far corner. He looked further. The building was huge. There was straw on the floor at his feet. He was in some sort of barn. He looked down himself. Naked. He covered his cock for a moment, then stopped. No one there to see. Focussing on the things pushed into the shadows, he could see the blanket that they'd used in the field. Yes. That was it. Then it all came back to him, flooding back in a wave. He stood. Barely able to stand upright with his hand chained to the wall. "Help," he called. "Help me, I'm in here." The words croaked from his dry mouth. Throat sore. He didn't know how long he'd been there. He reached up with his free hand and caressed his face. There was blood dried over it. His nose clicked when he touched it. Maybe broken. A lump across the bridge of it. His stomach turned in hunger, too. "Reggie?" he called out.

But apart from the sounds of the animals, there was no response.

So, he sat. And waited.

Maybe they'd taken her to the hospital. Her leg. Got it sewn back on. He started to sob big, wet tears. He leaned back against the wall and curled his legs up into his chest, wrapping himself within his arms, reliving the last holiday he would likely ever have.

Sobbing air out. Drowsy with exhaustion, and pain.

———

Richard opened his eyes to the sound of a bolt unlocking. The barn, suddenly full of light. He raised his head, pain dancing around inside it. He squinted at the attacking sunlight; his eyes not used to it. A shadow coming from the light. Silhouetted at first, and then the shape taken.

He breathed in through his nose a little, again. That smell. The barn was full of it. Animals and blood. Shit stink.

When the figure got closer, he could see it was Lewis. "Where am I? What have you done? Where's Reggie?"

"Reggie," the man said. "Ah, yes. The young lady." He continued across to the shadows, into the darkness. "Why she's right 'ere." Then he pulled the blanket from where it lay, out of the shadows in the corner of the barn. The blanket, something weighty inside it.

The sound of disturbed flies as they rose from the thick material, sodden with blood and gore. He pulled it into the light.

"Yes," he said. "You were roommates and you di'n't know it." He flicked the blanket back from her and let Richard see.

She was naked. Her chest ripped open by something. Leg missing. The other half hanging off. She was long dead and cold. Her eyes were open. Wide. Staring in fear.

"Why is she naked?" Richard asked. He couldn't think straight. He couldn't *feel*. She wasn't naked before, was she?

"Well," Lewis replied. "That's a story." He laughed. Looked down at her. "See, I like them young."

"No," Richard blurted. He was shaking his head, pulling himself tighter into a ball. "No. You didn't."

The older man nodded his head. "Oh, bu' I did." He seemed to say the words with such glee. "But that's not why she be naked. Old Daisy," he said.

"Daisy," Richard echoed dumbly.

"Yes. Daisy. She gets the craps when she has too much man-made material." He stooped down and took hold of the blanket again, dragging Reggie's corpse out of the barn door, into the sunlight while Richard stared on. Useless.

Then a chorus of pig squeals filled the barn from outside. A song of happy noises. One raised by such things that Richard could only imagine. The tears on his face, again. He didn't know what to do. He was … trapped. Why?

A few moments later, Lewis returned with the blanket rolled under his arm. He tossed it back into the darkness of the corner of the barn under the eye of Richard. Before Richard asked, "Why am I here?"

Lewis stopped what he was doing and turned and looked at him. "Well, that's the question, ain't it?" He grinned at Richard.

"You can't do this," he said. He knew the words were pathetic and meaningless.

"Can and 'ave," he said. "You can scream for 'elp and you can cry and stamp your feet, but it'll get you nowhere. Ain't nobody but family here." He turned to leave, but paused. "La'er on," he said, "we'll find out what youse really made of, and find out if we need to do this the easy way …" he turned, "or the 'ard way," closing the door behind him.

Richard stared into the darkness created by the door. Waiting for his eyes to adjust. What had happened? Why was *this* happening? Fuck. He rolled up onto his knees. He had to get out. He didn't want to find out what they had planned for him. He wanted to find the police and get the fuck out. And get them banged up for what they'd done. He pulled on the chain, wrapping it around his hand and yanking it, trying to break it free from the wall.

But it didn't so much as creak under all his weight. He slumped down and drew breath, waiting for his heart to stop beating quite so hard.

He wriggled around onto his arse. Looking around the straw beneath him. Fuck waiting. He was going to do something. He was going to get out. He stood. Testing how far he could reach with the chain still on.

Not far enough to reach anything. He stopped pulling and twisting and turning and closed his eyes, standing there naked. *Well*, he thought. *That's that*. He couldn't reach anything. Eyes back open. No. He turned back to the wall. The one he was chained to. Beyond the panel that was fixed to it. He felt around, reaching into gaps and crevices looking for something. Anything. He didn't even know what he was looking for. Just … he stopped and felt himself slump. His muscles relaxing into nothing. He could feel this desolate hate-filled despair taking a long hard grip on him.

He leaned against the wall and slid down to the floor. Fight, gone. He had to get from the clasp on his wrist. It was going to be his only way out. He looked at it. Locked shut. He'd seen films. Any fucking Joe could pick a lock in films, but he was pretty sure he couldn't. The clasp was tight to the wrist. It was like a jubilee clip—wrapped in on itself to create a perfect fit every time. He drew air in long and hard and let it out slowly. Fingers pushing under the metal, trying to do what, he didn't know. He rested his head back and let his arms and legs relax. He was so cold. Without the sunlight on him.

Tired. And hungry.

This wasn't how the driving holiday was supposed to go. He looked at the beams of light coming from the walls. He could tell the sun had moved a little since he paid attention last time. It must be afternoon. The sun beams getting lower. Probably the same day. He hadn't eaten breakfast on the promise of a glorious picnic. Got halfway through a shit pork pie. Maybe. His memory was so fuzzy. And all he could picture was her … there on the blanket. Him standing over her. The smell in the barn was dissipating. It had been her all along.

The sound of the flies gone.

C H A P T E R   7

A night had passed. Only one? He snorted, shivered at the same time. Christ. Richard wondered how long it was going to be before anyone even realised they were gone. His thoughts turned back to Reggie—again—and he let out a short sob. All he could see was her lifeless body under the blanket. Broken.

Dead.

He leant his head back, arms curled around him. They had another ten days of holidaying to do. Mostly nothing was booked—not that hotels cared if you didn't show. They'd just deduct the deposit and move right on. The hotel they were staying at? He shook his head subconsciously. No. They'd go up to the room and find half their clothes there, just pack the lot up in bin liners and stuff it in lost and found.

Maybe if someone saw the car sitting there on the side of the road. A policeman maybe? Someone might run the plates … but what did it matter? It wasn't illegally parked. It hadn't been reported stolen. Shit.

He thought about his phone. Sitting in the hotel room. Waiting on the rice that was still in the boot of the car.

Fuck.

He knocked his head against the wall behind him, trying to think his way out. It was all he had left. Hour after hour of thinking about how he should have acted differently. How he should have done *something*. When they acted sinisterly, he should have gotten to his feet. When they came across the field, he should have insisted they get up and … they should have left the day before, or that morning, and gone on somewhere else. Not cared about how fucking idyllic this place was. How nice. How …. *Fuck*. There was some noise from outside the barn. Sounded like animal movement.

Richard looked to the wall of the stalls to his side and shook his head. The cows are sleeping. He was pretty sure they were cows, anyway. Sounded like it.

He drew air in and shivered. Rubbed his hands over his skin, goose bumps raised hard. He needed to pee. He'd needed to several hours ago and he'd gotten shakily to his feet and peed out away from the wall, aiming it into the middle of the barn so it was nowhere near him. So he didn't have to sit near it. He could still smell it, though.

Another noise from outside. A door closing.

His piss disappeared back up into his body, and he froze, there on the spot. Waiting. Listening. Breath held.

There was a voice. Two of them. Talking. It sounded like him and her. The fucking farmers. Psycho and his psycho wife. The ones who had killed *his* wife.

He swallowed back the grief. Had to, in order not to make a sound.

The voices got louder. They were talking about benign bullshit. Fucking breakfast cereal. Their fucking kids. *Kids*. Then the barn door opened.

Lewis came in first. He had his shotgun cocked open—if that was the right word—over his arm again, like before. Then Maisie, she stood, silhouetted in the door, the bright, warm sun behind her. She leant against the door. Didn't speak, coming no closer, and not letting Richard see her properly.

Lewis came in, though.

He walked about halfway from the barn door to Richard before he stopped. Richard could see him, clearly framed with the sunshine behind him, making him look almost heavenly. "What do you want from me?" Richard rasped, his throat dry, hoarse.

Lewis nodded. "Still chained up I see." His words were quiet, creeping from his mouth. Darkness surrounded them, like it enveloped Maisie at the door.

"What the fuck did you think you were going to find?" Richards' words hissed from him, weakly, and tired.

"So," he said. Paced a few to the left and right like he was about to start this big speech. "My wife needs your 'elp," he said.

What the fuck? Richard focussed on the man, his pacing, his words. What the hell could Richard possibly offer? They were mad. That was it. *Mad.* Not psychopaths as he'd first assumed, but clinically insane.

"She's jonesing for 'nother child, you see, and I …" he stopped pacing. "… I can't. It's genetics, I guess. She be lookin' for a boy. You understand?"

Richard nodded. Of course he understood, *you fucking looney*. "What's this got to do with me?" He felt like he was just saying the words. He knew what was coming next, he just couldn not bring himself to believe it. It was like something out of a horror movie. A shit one at that.

"I need you to do …" Lewis rolled his free hand over, giving the 'and so on' gesture.

"What?" Richard needed him to say it. To *confirm* it.

"I want you to make my wife a chil'." His voice deepened further as he spoke. Richard could hear the hate and anger in the words.

"You want me to have sex with Maisie." Richard could feel the tears running down his face. Was this what this was all about? Is this why they'd killed Reggie? So he could *fuck* that ugly old fucking woman. Richard could feel himself becoming lightheaded. He could feel the world spin. "You want me to fuck her?" he whispered. Must have been loud enough for Lewis to hear, though.

"Youse not to enjoy it, you 'ear."

Richard partly snorted out a laugh, and partly choked. A little sob. "Not enjoy it." He dropped his head down onto his knees. "And then what?"

"What do you mean?" Lewis asked.

"Then what? Then what are you going to do to me?"

"We'll let youse go, of course."

Yeah, right. Just untie you and let you free. Give you your clothes back. Of course. It made sense. A small part of Richard wanted them to be mad enough to do just that. To give him his stuff and let him be free, but he didn't think they were *that mad*. They'd guarantee the pregnancy and then feed him to the pigs. "And what if I can't?" he asked quietly.

"We have preparations for tha'."

"Little blue pills, I suppose," Richard retorted without thinking.

"Oh no," Lewis boomed loudly. "We 'ave *the machine*."

Oh good. Richard squinted at the madman. "The machine?" He shouldn't have asked. He knew he shouldn't have asked.

"I like to watch …" Lewis stopped himself, looked like he was thinking about how to get the words out. "I like things." He seemed happier with those words, even if they didn't seem to make a bean of sense. "And I've learned things." He turned on his heel and faced Richard properly for the first time. "See, I'm no doctor."

No shit.

"But I knew what I needed to do the first time it 'appened."

This wasn't making any sense, the ramblings of a literal mad man.

"Cows," he boomed. "See, we milk cows."

Suddenly the words machine and milking stuck fast in Richard's head and with conscious thought he pulled on the chain, a sudden desire for freedom. The chain movement was enough to break the flow of the man's words, if only briefly.

"There are milking videos online." The volume dropped as he talked about his viewing preferences. "You know, where these ladies just do a man until … he," he paused. "So, I thought 'bout making the two of them a thing." He grinned, pleased with himself. "I might not be much of a medical man, but I know 'ow to seed a man. Youse know. If youse can't manage it for her." He turned away from Richard. "Although I don't know why any man wouldn't. She's a fine woman." Then back to face Richard. "Although, that doesn't solve the problem that you think you might have with needing those medicinal crutches. Can't get it up, aye? Well, I believe I can 'elp." He laughed. "Not li'erally," he said. He came a little closer. Like he wanted to share a secret. The two of them were close enough that they could look each other in the eyes. "Do you know what prostate milking is?" he whispered. "Then it don't matter if it's up." He winked at Richard.

Winked at him.

Then Lewis stood. "That's what the machine does. All of it at once." He turned back. To punctuate. "If you can't … get … it … up."

Richard was staring at him. He had this picture in his mind of a fucking machine. Some teet milker strapped to his cock while a motorised dildo reamed his arsehole. *Prostrate.* The fucking absurdity. Farmer fucking Giles here standing over him, laughing, saying *good*, like a goddamn Star Wars villain. He wanted to blurt out that he couldn't have kids. He didn't know if he could or not, they'd never tried, but he thought it might stop all this … but then he'd be useless to them. He'd be inconsequential. He'd be chicken feed.

Lewis waved Maisie into the barn, out of the light, so he could show her off. Like Richard hadn't seen the bitch before. She came and stood next to Lewis. She was smiling like they were fucking prom dates. "How 'bout it?" she said.

It was as if the two crazies thought this was some negotiation. Even after the threats. The murder. The body disposal. "Yeah," Richard said. He didn't feel like he was left with a choice. Fuck her or die. Or the machine. He wasn't sure what was worse. He looked Maisie up and down. Horrified at the thought.

But without an option.

"Good," said Lewis. "We'll get star'ed in a while."

The two of them turned to leave, going to the door and closing it, slicing off the light and the warmth of the sun, leaving Richard there, sitting and staring into the darkness, broken only by the shards of light breaking through the wall.

"Well, this is going to be interesting."

Richard looked at Reggie and then back at the

door. "Yeah."

"How are you supposed to," she cleared her throat, "without enjoying it? Isn't that part of the performance?"

Richard looked at her. One leg gone. The other was a mess. Her torso bust open like a trodden on tomato. "It is."

Cow movement took his attention. "It is." When he looked back, she was gone.

C H A P T E R   8

Shirley held on around Danny's waist. He was riding too fast—not that she didn't like the feeling of the speed, but rather, the country lanes were pretty narrow and she didn't particularly want to end up smooshed into the front of a tractor. Dying young and leaving a good-looking corpse was one thing, but she was pretty sure this wasn't what they meant.

The bike dipped to the side as they turned and she leant with it. If you leant against it and tried to stay upright, you died.

Then up, out of the bend. Around a slow-moving car. She patted him on the shoulder. "When are we stopping?" she shouted over the noise of the machine.

"Next town," he replied.

No idea of the inflection in his voice. Could have been stopping on a whim, could have been stopping because she asked. He broke hard and she gripped tighter. Then accelerated, the front wheel leaving the road by a few inches as they sped away.

Gripped even tighter.

Her stomach turned. Not because of the lift,

although that was there, but because of the fear of falling. With her on the back, surely it would be so easy to over balance, tip backwards. The last thing she wanted was to land on her back on the road with him and the bike between her legs.

Then the bike dropped back, and he dropped a gear. The roar of the engine quieting as he slowed the thing down. He nodded toward … something … the bike suddenly slowing and then hitting a corner, around, into an even smaller road—if you could call it that.

Shirley saw a sign for a town whizz past. Could have been anywhere. No way of seeing with it passing by like that so suddenly.

They whipped around a cyclist, an old woman, one of those bikes that had three gears and a basket on the front. At least they must be close to something. Those bikes didn't do cross-country. She smiled to herself as they went over a small humpbacked bridge, before suddenly entering a village.

The bike rolling, coasting, to a stop on the side of the road. He killed the engine, and she stepped off. She could feel the ache of hours on a bike in her knees—not like she was old enough to feel that yet—and the judder on her back. The vibrations making everything feel funny now they'd stopped.

She pulled the helmet off and finally felt the air on her head. Unzipped the leather jacket, letting it flop open. It was hot in there when you stopped moving. Danny stepped from the bike, rolling his hands in his gloves. He pulled them and his helmet off, letting his long brown hair out. It clung to his neck with sweat. He smiled at her. "Time for a break," he said.

"What time is it?" she asked, looking around the village. Old, decaying buildings everywhere. It looked like it hadn't seen an update in years.

Danny yanked his hand forward and got his watch out from his sleeve. "Eleven." He hooked his helmet over the handlebars and strode back and forth a little, working the aches out. "Got lucky with the weather." He was looking up.

Shirley wondered why he had so little to say. They'd only been dating a few weeks, and he always seemed so … bored … of her. She glanced up. "Very nice," she said. "Hungry?"

Nodding, he took her hand. Gestured to the bike with the other. She placed her helmet on the other side of the handlebars. "The helmets gonna be all right here?" she asked as he led her away.

"It doesn't look much like Midsommer," he said.

She didn't get the reference, but she didn't always. He was a few years her senior, and he had so much more life experience.

He led her down the street, looking at the doors and in the front gardens. He seemed taken by the houses.

"I like the buildings," she said, trying to engage him.

He grunted a response, which she thought might be all she was going to get. "Food?" she said, again.

"Here," he said. He pointed up the street to the pub.

"Bit early, isn't it?" she said. She really didn't want to get on the back of that thing if he was going to have a drink.

"We can get something to eat in there, yeah?" he pulled her on, like he was desperate to get there.

The Frog and Bucket. He paused, the two of them looking at the sign. Hand painted amphibian and bucket with a hole in it. "Nice," he said. Pulled her in.

Shirley followed him in obediently. Danny let her go and she went to the seats. Like he'd done in all the pubs they'd been in this last week. He went to the bar and ordered. It seemed to be the way he liked to do things.

She sat on the banquet seating next to a table and watched him. He went to the bar. Young barmaid. Pretty. She was flirty. Shirley could tell before she even spoke to Danny that she was going to throw herself at him. She blinked it away. He probably wasn't like that, though. She looked up at the TV. On. Sound off. There were the morning shows on. Just finishing up. No good without the sound. A pool table with a stained baize. Dartboard with the darts sticking out of it.

The bimbo behind the bar laughed, and Shirley snapped her look to her. She *was* flirting. She glanced at Shirley, and she could almost feel the look of disdain. Shirley glanced down at herself. Her t-shirt under her leather jacket had a deep stain around the neck from sweat. Her hair was probably a state. Fuck.

She looked around the bar for a bathroom. Something with a mirror. The single overnight bag they were carrying was tucked into the panniers of the bike. Shit. She should have brought it.

Danny turned from the bar and brought a couple of pints over, putting them on the table and sitting.

"Drinking?" she said. She tried to sound like she wasn't nagging. Didn't want a barney in the middle of the pub. He nodded his response, already having the glass to his lips. "She seemed nice," Shirley said. It was passive aggressive but fuck it.

He was still nodding when he took the glass from his lips. "We can stay here tonight," he said. "They do a B and B. only thirty-nine quid."

Shirley gazed over to the barmaid, garnering a glance back, the two of them meeting eyes, and the barmaid smiled. "I'll bet," she whispered.

"What's up?" he asked, oblivious.

Of course he was oblivious. He was a man.

"Do I look all right?" she asked.

"Gorgeous," he said. Without looking.

It was nice to say and all, but he could pretend to look. She shook her head and picked up the pint he'd brought for her. A sip. Strong. "Nice," she said.

"Local," he responded.

Jesus, it was like dating Shakespeare. "Food?" she asked.

"Coming."

Shirley looked up at the barmaid. She wasn't making anything to eat. Maybe there was someone in the back? Her eyes wandered to the TV again. News playing now. Something about an accident somewhere. Motorway closed. Then her look dropped to Danny. "So, are we staying here for the rest of the day?" She glanced around the pub.

"After lunch, we can take in the town. Back here for dinner. And then bed." He winked at her.

She hated that he was so sexy when he wanted to be and such a theologian the rest of the time. She coughed the laugh away. It wasn't his mind she'd hooked up with. It was his body. They both knew that. And besides … a night in a quaint little town in the middle of nowhere? Should make for a nice break from all the riding they seemed to be doing.

C H A P T E R   9

Tim forked his pork chop, shovelling it into his mouth and chewing without manners nor concern for them. He chewed, eyeing his mother and father on the other side of the table and giving the occasional look to Anton.

Anton had his knife and fork in a death gripp, resting on the handles either side of his plate. "Another one," he said. The disdain was clear.

"It's what youse mother wants," Lewis said.

"I don't get it." His eyes stayed fast on Maisie, watching her, but apparently getting his answers from the person next to her.

"It's not youse concern."

"Oh, but it is," he hissed, taking his utensils and attacking his roasted potatoes.

The four of them sat around the kitchen table, the room full of the smells of a midweek roast. A quick one. Packet gravy. That sort of thing. Maisie had even used frozen roast potatoes.

"Have you heard from Jean?" Tim asked, seeing if

he could change the subject.

"Oh yes," said Maisie, now allowed to speak for herself. "She said she would try to get down for a visit soon."

"I don't understand why you want to keep another man in the barn," Anton said, too loudly.

Everybody knew what he meant. He meant *have another baby*. Another sibling. Someone to potentially cause a problem down the line when it came to farm ownership and taking over.

Maisie drew in a breath as the silence fell over the table. Even Lewis didn't say anything.

"That'll be nice," Tim mumbled, trying to keep the conversation on track.

"Won't it." Maisie shoved a carrot into her mouth, taking her ability to talk. Her eyes on Anton.

Anton shoved his knife and fork down next to his plate like a petulant child. He pushed his chair back, scraping it over the old, tiled floor, and sat there, pensive for a moment.

Tim watched as it looked like Lewis might spring to his feet and give Anton a piece of his mind, or alternatively, the back of his hand, as was his wont on some occasions.

Anton had always been the one to start it. Verbally, of course. Anton wasn't a fighter. Neither was Tim. They were both far too foppish for that sort of horseplay, but Anton had a way with his words, his slight actions, a way of getting on the wrong side of

Lewis. Lewis was a brute. Always had been. It made him a good farmer, at least, to be heartless, and a heathen. To tend to animals one minute and send them to market the next. Something Tim had never relished. He supposed it was the reason he was trying to escape the life, much as Jean had. She'd achieved things he could only dream of.

Tim looked to Anton, staring at his father. Lewis staring back, chewing, mouth open. The look of *dare* in his eyes. Then he looked at his mother. She looked tired, in all fairness. Not youthful, not the sort of look he expected for a woman trying to mother again. To give them another brother, or perhaps, another sister. Tim wouldn't mind another sister. He rather enjoyed Jean.

Anton stood, taking Tim from his thoughts. "This family," he said.

Lewis rose too, but Maisie put her hand on his and stopped him. He was going to throw himself across the room, Tim was sure, before she tamed him. She had always been able to. But she didn't. Hadn't, at least. Many times, in the past, she'd let Lewis throw fists into the two of them. Show them who's boss. Show them who the leader of the pack is. Let the boys have it out.

And Lewis had never once lost that fight.

Tim looked down at himself, then to his brother. Lewis couldn't lose a fight to the two of them if he tried.

Anton threw his serviette down, having taken it from his lap, onto his plate, and then stormed to the door. Opened it. He stopped and looked back, perhaps surprised that he wasn't stopped. Then out. Slamming the heavy wooden door behind him.

Tim saw the slam coming, but he still jumped when the noise filled the room.

Maisie was rubbing the back of Lewis's hand, trying to calm the beast. Tim glanced, but nothing more than a glance, to his father's eyes, seeing the roar of the animal there. The fire and brimstone. The ruler of the house without question.

Anton was likely to pay for his digression later, when Maisie wasn't there to stop it. Anton would know that already, but his anger at losing his place in the hierarchy was more powerful. Tim shook his head and chewed. The pork tasted nice, but it was a little tough. It wasn't like Anton had lost anything, but he would, if he continued like that. Lewis wouldn't allow his protégé to behave in such a childish and stubborn manner. Likely, Anton would hold his hopes of getting a sister too, for different reasons to Tim.

"And wha' are youse looking at?"

Tim hadn't realised that his eyes had fallen back on his father and while he was staring at nothing in particular, he could tell his father thought he was looking at him. "Sorry," he said. "Miles away."

"Fuck," Lewis replied.

Tim was surprised his father hadn't used the slur he was so fond of these days. He looked down into his plate. Not as hungry as he was three minutes ago before this all started, with the innocuous question from Anton about why they'd spent so much time in the barn that day, and was one of the cows sick? It was loaded, because they both knew exactly why their parents had been in the barn. He scooped peas. He liked peas. Looked over to this mother without looking like he was looking over to her. She had a lump of veg on her knife. Speared through it. She was looking out the kitchen window. From there, all she would be able to see was the sky.

He wondered why she stared at the sky.

Then Lewis thumped a closed fist down on the table, and everyone and everything jumped slightly. Snapped back to the silence of the room, and Lewis, sitting back down. He angrily cut through his food and shoved it into his mouth like it was suddenly a chore.

"And when your sister gets 'ere," he said, spitting globs of food out from his mouth, "youse be nice to her."

Tim nodded. "Yes, Dad." Of course he would.

C H A P T E R   1 0

Shirley giggled uncontrollably as Danny pulled her from the small corridor down the back of the bar into the gents bathroom. It was less of a bathroom and more of a cubicle, but if you could get two people inside…He pushed her against the wall and closed the door too loudly, the crack of wood on wood, he pushed the bolt across. Turned back to her and crushed his mouth into hers. Hard and desperate. He needed her. Right then. After sinking a few beers, and talking about shit, and whatever, he *needed* her.

"But we have the room upstairs," she said, as he pulled away from her.

"I don't care," he growled. He pulled her jacket open over her shoulders, trapping her arms down by her side. Dropping to his knees in front of her, and pulled her shirt up, kissing her stomach. Her breathing becoming slower, more defined, the giggling stopping. He slipped her bra up, over her breasts, and used his mouth to enjoy them, too, his eyes persistently roaming up her to hers, meeting them. Fucking her with them. She watched him, his touch firing electricity through her. She could feel him working her jeans down as he pleased her with his tongue. Then he stood, turned her to face the wall, and she could feel him free his own jeans. Feel his cock hard and against her as his lips found crevices in her neck to kiss and bite. She shuddered as he entered her.

His desperate need to be with her was more of a turn-on than he could possibly imagine. He grunted in her ear, his hot breath warming as her body pushed against the wall. She drove her hips back to give him the access he needed for depth, and then let him plough into her, deep and hard. Her grunts joined his as she felt an orgasm bloom inside her. She parted her legs further, trying to get more of him as his thrusts became more urgent and the two of them found a motion, "A little more," she said. Low and quiet between grunts. "Just there," she continued as he pushed harder.

Deeper.

The orgasm flushed over her and she shuddered, a small whine escaping her lips as she tightened every muscle she had, and then he came, deep inside her. Letting out a long sigh as he relaxed, stood there, his arms snaking around her, pulling her in close to him, his fingers discovering her body, running over her while the two of them glowed together.

Danny reached over for the toilet paper and pulled a handful off, giving it to her, before pulling himself from her. She pushed the toilet roll between her legs, and turned, kissing him deeply. The two held there for a moment.

Shirley dropped away from the kiss, and leaned back against the sink, still breathing hard, as Danny pushed himself back in his jeans. "Go on," she said.

"Then we can go to the room. Watch some TV, yeah?"

He nodded and turned out of the bathroom. Leaving her to clean herself up. Both of them sated.

Which she did, quickly. Only needed to be quick. The room that Danny had gotten had a shower, thankfully. She wiped herself over and flushed the toilet paper. Then got another handful and stuffed it into her panties, before pulling up her jeans and securing them. That would get her to the shower without leaking on her clothes.

It had only taken a minute.

She left the bathroom and went to the bar. Danny was leaning up against it talking to the barmaid. He was perched on the stool. Elbows on the bar. Leaning forward. "You coming?" she called.

He glanced back. Then she saw he had a fresh pint. "You go ahead. I'm just having another."

She stared at him for a moment, before shaking her head as he turned back. The fucking barmaid was looking over his shoulder at her. She had one of those little flirtatious smiles on her face. *Bitch*.

Shirley turned away and went from the bar to the stairs and up. "Fucker," she muttered, exasperated that Danny could fuck her and then be all over some tart only a minute later. She was going to … she stopped herself, feeling the drip of cum in her panties. She was going to have a shower first, that was what she was going to do, but if he thought he was getting another quickie in the stall of some shitty pub again, he had another thing coming. She slammed the door to their room and slammed the door to the bathroom.

———

Danny leaned forward a little more. This chick behind the bar had made it clear that she knew what the two of them had been up to in the shitter, but she was still throwing herself at him. That was fine. Christ, he couldn't even remember her name. He was fairly sure she had given it to him. He glanced around the empty pub. Maybe this was why she was doing it. Just for something to do? She leaned forward a little. It was very practised. Letting him see down her top, just a little. Tease.

He was too old for that shit, but he looked anyway. Sometimes you have to play the game. He gave her a sly smile when he saw her watch him look. The game. "Always this quiet?" he asked.

"Sometimes, yeah. Midweek, innit."

He nodded. "You work here every night?"

"Most of them, yeah. I can take time off whenever though. Close up even." She seemed impressed with herself that she was entrusted to lock up an empty pub. "Why?" Her look was something more than inquisitiveness.

Danny almost laughed at her, but it wasn't the time. He covered it, picking up his pint and taking a sip. "Just wondered what you did for fun."

"This is it, baby." She wiggled trying to be provocative. It would probably work on the hicks that lived around these parts, but classy, she wasn't.

"You?" he raised his eyebrows. Smiled.

She laughed. "No silly, the pub."

"Oh," he said, nodding.

"You're teasing me," she said. "You think I'm dumb."

Danny couldn't tell if she was joking or flirting or if she really was dumb. He shook his head, playing along. "No, of course not." The smile widened. Practised, again. Still. He was sure this broad had no idea about … well *anything*. Ever. He sipped his beer again. "Oh," he said, "I'm sorry, can I get you one?"

She shook her head and looked him down. Only a glance, but she was definitely checking him out.

She certainly was coming across as the girl who only had fun when she was trying to get laid, which was fine. "So, you get many out of towners?"

"Some," she said, dismissively.

He could tell she wasn't interested in small talk. Tough shit. "Recently?"

She raised her eyes and looked at the ceiling. "I guess." She pushed her chest out. That was what some women did, using their bodies to get what they wanted.

He was losing her interest, so he made sure she saw him admiring her. "Many bikers?" he asked, just as absently.

"One or two," she leaned down, forward.

She was unbelievable. His missus was in the room upstairs. She was literally trying to lay a guy who'd just poked his girl in the bathroom. And she knew it.

"I like a biker," she said.

Danny pushed his fingers into his leather. "Good," he said, pulling his wallet. He opened it and took out a ten, put it on the bar for his beer. Then he took a photo out. He showed it to her. "You seen this biker recently?"

C H A P T E R   1 1

Tim stood at the barn door, leaning against it. The man in the barn was watching him. The two of them stood in the twilight watching each other in silence. The man hadn't spoken once. He was just there. Anton, surprised that the man hadn't immediately begged for his life, had bored quickly and was over at the pigs, talking with them. He enjoyed talking with the pigs for some reason. Perhaps he felt like he got more sense from them than from his parents.

And maybe he did.

"So," he said, addressing the man. "You are to sire my next sibling."

The man nodded. "Apparently so."

It wasn't the first time Tim had come to the barn to taunt one of his mother's … suitors … but this one seemed a little more civil than some. He snorted into his wine. The man slowly turns into a shadow in the half light. The night becoming deeper. Tim walked into the doorway, into the darker barn, to allow his eyes to get used to the light, and to be able to see him better. "What do you do for a living?"

The man laughed. A gentle, dinner party laugh. "Really?" he said.

"I want to know what sort of stock you're from, of course."

"Stock," the man mumbled.

Tim got closer. The man didn't try to hide himself, his nakedness. "Oh," he said, looking between Richard's legs. "I hope we get a girl for their sake." He shook his head.

The man turned his body. "It's not what you've got," he said. "It's what you do with it."

Tim laughed loudly. "I see we're practised with that come back."

"Fuck you."

"That's better."

"Stop playing with him," Anton said. "Mum and dad are coming."

Tim turned. Anton in the door of the barn. "Laters," he said, absently to the man, before wandering to his brother. No sense in hiding the fact they were there. Their parents, halfway across the yard. Mother was dressed sexy. She was in a kimono thing, high heels. It made her look stupid, so Tim thought. He watched her totter like a cheap prossie across the farmyard, with her husband next to her.

"And what are youse two doin'?" he asked. "Be'er not be scarin' the animals."

Tim shook his head. "Oh no, Father, just admiring

the stock." He smiled, smug. Hopefully, over his father's head.

"Youse two get in now."

Anton didn't speak. He was already half wandering in the direction of the house, with absolutely no intention of getting into anything with his father again. Tim raised his glass in a toast and followed.

Then Lewis turned to his wife. "Youse ready, lass?"

She smiled. "I am. To be a mum again."

"You know those boys dote on youse, and their sisters, youse know, if youse didn't want to we could always …" he paused, "… get a dog." She frowned, and he knew she had her mind set. "Come on," he said, leading her into the barn.

——

Richard watched the young man with the wine glass leave. There was a conversation outside the barn door but couldn't hear.

Reggie said, "You gonna manage it?"

He glanced to her. "Sure," he lied.

"You know they'll kill you if you don't."

"I don't need the extra pressure."

"Hallo my loverly," said Maisie, coming into the barn.

Richard looked from her to Reggie, who was now gone, and back again. She looked like a pig in makeup. Stupid fucking woman. The man, Lewis, stood at the door and waited. Like a fucking bouncer in a strip joint. He'd only ever visited one strip joint, and remarkably, this particular venue was seedier. At the time, he doubted he could have gotten any lower in life, but here he was. Chained naked in a barn with a dead wife and a horny bitch and her cuck fucking husband.

She stopped the totter and stood there, in front of him for a moment, probably for effect. It *was* having an effect, but probably not the one she wanted. He was feeling nauseous. Then she opened the robe she was wearing.

Beneath, she had on a lacey, strappy, thing that didn't fit well. It was too small. Richard had absolutely nothing against any particular shaped woman—he'd always truthfully maintained that it was more about the person than the body, which is why he'd never been one to collect notches on bedposts—but this wasn't attractive. She was mutton, dressed as lamb. She exuded desperation. A need for a younger man to satisfy her.

Richard looked around her. To Lewis. "Is he going to watch?" he asked, trying to find some reason—any reason—to not have to deal with … her.

"Only in case you try to do somethin' silly." She dropped the robe from her shoulders and stood there in the darkness, clearly impressed with herself. "Just ignore him."

"Cuck," Richard said, loud enough for Lewis to

hear. Although he probably wouldn't have a clue what it meant.

"Do I dows it for yow?" Maisie asked, getting his attention back to her.

He looked at her. No. Most certainly not. If he'd been single and out drinking, she might have garnered a second look, but chained in the barn, dead wife, cuckold husband, starving hungry. Depleted of water. There were numerous reasons that she didn't … *do it for him*. But what was going to be worse? Not doing it, or doing it? If he did it, they had no reason to keep him alive, although looking at what he had to do to do it, he might prefer death at that point—and not doing it was going to incur the wrath of *the machine*. Whatever that contraption was. It surely wouldn't work. This Neanderthal man couldn't build a human milking machine, surely? Fuck. That was right. Lewis said he'd had an appetite for online porn. So, he was probably reeling from the cuck jibe. Maisie dropped the straps from her bra over her shoulders and watched Richard, looking for a reaction.

"Yeah," he said. It wasn't like they would kill him tonight, was it? They'd have to confirm success first. He rolled his body around and got to his knees. He wasn't enjoying it, and his body told her that. But she was going to have to do more than tease him to get that going in these circumstances. *Come on*, he thought. He needed to get hard.

Lewis wasn't helping.

She pulled the bra from her body, standing there in heels and panties. She looked ridiculous. "You wanna fuck me?" she said, her voice low, and trying to be sexy.

"Yeah," he said, again. His usual charm gone. He looked down her body. Willed his body to respond to hers.

She stepped closer. Within reach. Whispered, "Now don't you do nothin' silly, or my 'usband will kill you." Then she turned and presented her arse to his face.

Richard glanced down at himself, unmoved by it, as it were. He closed his eyes and tried to imagine something … anything … else. But he could smell her now. She didn't smell bad. He'd imagined a *farmer* smell, but she was washed down in cheap perfume. It all felt like a cheap, like a back-alley whore. He opened his eyes to find her peeling her underwear off, inches from his face, that string bit at the back of a g-string pulling from between her arse crack. It was the single most un-sexy thing that could have happened. He closed his eyes again. Tight. Praying that this was all a nightmare and he was going to wake up on the blanket having had one too many glasses of wine and passed out, with Reggie, there by his side.

"It doesn't work like that," Reggie said.

Richard opened his eyes. That woman was gyrating. He looked to the side. Reggie. Watching him get his nasty on with the farmer woman. "What?" he hissed.

"Waking up and finding it was all dream." She nodded to Maisie. "You gonna have to do something about that, there."

Richard turned his attention back to Maisie. At least she had stopped the sexy dancing. She turned. "Why ain't youse touchin' me?" she asked. Loud enough for her husband to hear, of course.

"Sorry," Richard prattled. He stood, trying to decide what to … grab.

But Maisie reached forward and put her hand around his flaccid cock. "You not ready, lover?" she asked.

Richard wanted to puke. Even her touching him didn't raise a spark. He needed medical intervention. He wasn't going to get hard for this … woman. "Sorry," he mumbled again and then grabbed her breasts. They were large and comely. He squeezed them about like a teenager not knowing what he was doing, but she seemed to revel in it. She grabbed and twisted his cock, also like someone who didn't know what they were doing.

"Oh, yes," she said. "Dick by name …" She left the words to hang there.

Richard glanced over to Lewis. He had a flat cap on covering his eyes in shadow. Watching. Richard was sure he was just waiting for a reason. He looked down to find Maisie bending forward and gobbling his cock into her mouth.

Slobbering over it. Pulling back and forth.

It was no good. Nothing was going to get him hard. Richard closed his eyes. "Yeah baby," he said. He felt it sounded too Austin Powers and the sheer ridiculousness of the situation got the better of him, and he snorted out a laugh.

She pulled from him. "Why ain't youse 'ard?" she said.

Richard looked to Lewis, who had straightened in the doorway. Excuse found. It didn't help, and what little blood may have found its way into his penis, waved a white flag and retreated.

"God damn it," she screamed. "I thought youse were different."

She stepped away slightly and Richard noted that Lewis was already halfway to him.

Richard backed away into the wall. Hands up, passively. "No," he said. "I want to," he said.

"But?" Lewis said, moving between them.

Richard looked at Maisie. She looked honestly distraught. But Richard could find as much sympathy for her as he could sexual want. None. "I can't," he said.

"Fucker," Lewis replied. He drew his hand back, stepping into Richard and laying a fist hard into his gut.

The air gone from inside him, Richard stumbled back, crashing against the wall of the barn. His diaphragm unable to pull air back and forth, he made a sound like a blocked drain and curled over, his hands clutched into his gut like it might help. Lungs burned. A ring of black circled his vision. He could see Maisie in the middle of it. She was shying away, pulling her clothes from the floor. *No*, he thought. He wanted another go. Well, he supposed, needed more than wanted. Of course he didn't *want* to fuck her. How could they even think he could? But was willing to try, just to avoid the machine.

Lewis brought his hand up and swung. His hand collided with Richard's exposed face. He didn't even see it coming. Head snapped to the side. Blood spitting out. His neck cracked; pain lurched through it. His face, surprisingly numb.

Then it came.

He dropped to one knee. Felt the heat of his blood blooming on his face as it trickled from his lip, split and fattening. He even swallowed some back, tasting the iron within. Brain bouncing around in there. The world spinning. He waited, blinking away the shakes that seemed to suddenly grip him. Head thumping. Barely registering what had happened, Lewis punched him hard in the face again. White sparks of fire rose in Richard's vision and he thought he cried out, but everything sounded so lame. So dull. He wasn't a fighter. Never had been. Someone laying *the smackdown* on him was a new thing.

He was a nice boy.

He reached up and felt the side of his head. The darkness of the barn replacing the white light in his vision. He could see the shadows of Maisie and Lewis leaving. She looked upset. He couldn't think straight. There was a pang of guilt at not being able to perform, settling there in his gut. His fingers probing the egg shape that had already started to form on the side of his face. He looked at the darkness. The barn door closing.

The rise of the sounds of the cows in the next stall. He dropped back into the straw. Numb from the neck up. From the neck down, he hurt. The jar of the blows. The air only just finding its way back into his lungs.

He turned on the straw. Vomit rising from within.

He puked, just there, where he lay.

———

Daisy stood in the pen watching as the master and his wife left the building empty handed. Shame. She was hungry for something other than this swill that the master's son had given her for food. She wanted the flesh.

C H A P T E R   1 2

"What the fuck do you think you're playing at?"

Danny looked surprised at Shirley. He closed the door to the bedroom, slowly and quietly. Purposefully. He didn't want to be heard. "What?" he hissed back. Shirley was so passive most of the time. He hadn't expected the outburst. She was sitting on the bed, dressed, not naked as he'd expected in his welcome. Crossed legged. Danny could tell when a woman had been stewing on something, and she certainly had ever since she'd come back up here. Maybe she hadn't gotten what she wanted downstairs? Well, she was going to have to do better than this if she wanted him to make it up to her. Like *that*.

"You fuck me and then you're back at the bar before you've even gone soft trying to pick *her* up?"

Danny shot a look at the door. Damn. The last thing he needed was to raise the attention of the locals. Even the bartender downstairs. He strode to the bed, and put his hand up, like he might clamp it over her mouth, then thought better of it. "Just hush," he said, trying to control his temper.

"I saw you," she said, not hushing.

He raised a finger. "Listen," he said. "It's not like that." The sincerity in his voice seemed to calm her. "But do you mind if I shower quick?"

She stared into his eyes for a moment, then nodded, silently.

Danny dropped his jacket from his shoulder and to the floor inside the bedroom door, then he went into the bathroom. Didn't bother shutting the door. He certainly didn't have anything to hide. Not from her. He peeled his clothes off and got under the water, still freshly hot from her shower. He stood there, letting it run over him. Run off him. Thinking about her downstairs and what she'd said. What she'd *seen*.

He cleaned his junk off, and stepped out, dried quickly before wrapping a towel around himself and returning to the bedroom. Shirley had put the small TV on, quiet, and was on the bed. She'd stripped to her underwear. Clearly a little more comfortable than before.

Danny bent down and pulled his jacket from the floor. Got the photo out and rounded the bed and slipped down next to her. He handed it to her.

Shirley took it. "Nice looking boy," she said, almost dismissively. Then she looked at it a little longer. "Looks like you."

Danny nodded, taking the picture back and placing it carefully down on the bedside table. "My little brother," he said.

"So?" She was looking at the TV, but it was clear questions were starting to go around in her head.

Danny leant back on the headboard. Found some spot halfway up the wall to focus on. He hated even *telling* people he had a brother. Let alone this. "He went missing four weeks ago." He felt her look at him. Probably trying to judge if he was telling the truth. Well, he was. "I've been following the trail for three weeks now. It's led me here."

Shirley turned on the bed. "What?"

"When I met you … I wasn't in that bar looking for a lay, or you. I was looking for a geezer called Jerome, who apparently had been riding with Rob. I was looking for information."

"Rob," she echoed quietly.

"Yeah. Good kid. Wouldn't hurt a fly. Also, wouldn't go a week without calling his mum."

"What's happened to him?"

This was why he didn't like telling people things. In a desperate attempt to say something, they always sounded like they weren't listening. "I don't know, now do I?"

"Was that what you were doing with her? Trying to find out information?"

Danny nodded. "Yeah."

"And? Don't leave me hanging."

"She saw him a few weeks back. Said he flew into town alone." Danny was still focused on the wall. But after the two of them had spent the night together, she didn't see him again. "She said the last thing she saw was his bike, parked out near the church on the lane.

I'll head down there tomorrow and see what I can find."

"I'll come too, obviously. Why didn't you tell me?" Shirley's voice was quieter now. Gentler. She was suddenly in a different place, no longer full of suspicion. She put her hand up and cupped his chin, thumb on his lips as he watched the wall. "We'll find him."

Danny felt her hand start to remove the towel. He wasn't in the mood for that. Not now. He was going to find his brother. He was just worried that now, after four weeks, he might not find him how he wanted to. Three weeks ago, he expected to find him holed up in some fucking seaside town, doped up to the eyeballs, having gone off the rails over some bird and taking a cocktail of shit that stopped him from knowing what day it was. Now, he'd followed the scent halfway across the country, through God only remembered how many biker bars, to here. A fucking row of houses in the middle of bumfuck nowhere. Still, if he found his bike here, at least there was some hope. Maybe he'd just shacked up with some farmer's daughter.

Maybe.

Shirley had rolled over and had stuck his cock in her mouth, making him hard.

Oh well. Looked like he was in the mood for that, after all.

C H A P T E R   1 3

The cold bit into Richard's flesh. The night was harsh. He lay balled in the straw, wrapped in himself. He was hoping that if he fell asleep, one of two things would happen. Maybe he'd just sleep the night through. Wake up refreshed, and perhaps a little warmer. The other was that maybe he would freeze to death. Right there in the straw.

"Don't say that."

Richard opened his eyes. Teeth chattering. "Why not?" he muttered, the air coming from his mouth thick and white. "Why not?" he repeated, looking up at her. She was sitting in what would have been the cross-legged pose, but without her leg. The straw below her was sticky with blood.

"Because. Think of all the reasons you have to live."

He straightened, looking at her, then pushed himself to sit. "I'm looking at the only reason I had to live. And now I don't have one."

She shook her head. "Don't say that. People depend on you. You have an important job. Your mum and dad. They rely on you, don't they? And that fox in the back garden."

Richard shook his head. Thumping both sides as the blood, thickened by the cold, oozed about. "Whatever."

"Then for me," she said. "You need to live to help me. I'm pig feed, Richard. You need to stop them. Get justice. Vengeance. Something."

He stared at her. His heart aching to see her like that. Even in the darkness he could see she was paler. Deader. She was broken and drained, and … starting to smell. "Vengeance," he said, nodding. "Yeah. I understand that."

"I want you to get it, as well."

He looked at her, and she was grinning. "But you're not really here, are you?"

"Technically," she said, pointing to her own temple, "I'm here." Then her finger moved to her heart. "And here."

He nodded.

"Besides," she continued, "forgetting all that, that Lewis bloke says you're getting the machine now."

Richard rested his head back on the wall behind him, arms curled over his goose-bumped flesh. Rubbing back and forth. "Yeah."

"And he said what, milking and prostate?" She snorted. "You always said you wanted to be adventurous in the bedroom."

Richard rested his head forward onto his knees. "Not like that. I can only image what monstrosity he's concocted."

"Maybe we shouldn't find out."

Richard looked at her. "That sounds just lovely. You have an idea how?"

"Not really. I was hoping you do."

Richard closed his eyes. Tried not to think about the machine, even though that was what he seemed to be thinking about most. He could imagine, this thing with a cow's udder grabber on one end and a dildo on a pole on the other, designed to attack both ends at once and *milk* the subject. Jesus Christ.

"I wonder if he lubes?" she said.

Richard looked up and she was gone. Just her voice hanging in the air. He brought his hand to the side of his head and pressed gently, the pain spiking into him. Overriding the cold that numbed him. The tips of his fingers hurt. He wondered if he got frostbite or something, if they'd let him go. And by letting him go, he meant killing him without using the machine. Damaged goods and all that. He looked down at himself. Hadn't even been there that long and dehydration was starting to show in his flesh.

"They're going to kill you after they've taken your seed."

Richard looked up again, Reggie sitting there. "I know."

"They'll not keep you alive until conception has

been assured. That means that if they strap you into the machine tomorrow, then they'll probably kill you tomorrow."

Richard frowned. "You're not telling me anything I don't already know." He dropped his head back down to his knees and kept rubbing, hoping the blood would flow. He did know that. But there was no way he could get from this fucking chain.

C H A P T E R   1 4

Anton was staring out the window. From the vantage in his bedroom, he could see the lanes approaching the farm, the cool morning sunlight dancing shadows as the trees moved.

There was a car coming. He glanced over to Tim, who was still in bed. Then back out the window. Who could it be? He tapped, irritably, on the window frame. The cold came through the single-paned window.

"Stop that," Tim said, turning over.

Anton shook his head and headed from the bedroom to the landing, giving Tim little more than a glance. He headed downstairs. There was a smell of bread coming from the kitchen. It filled the house like a plague. Fresh and warming.

It was never a good sign if mother was baking.

He listened to the clatter of baking trays and the rise of the word *bollocks*, coming from the kitchen, so he bypassed it and went to the front door. Out into the yard. Watching the lane that came to the house. The gate open. The tractor was gone from where father had left it last night and he was off in the fields somewhere, clearly.

Anton glanced back at the house. He could see
mother in the kitchen. She paid him no mind but had a
face like thunder. Something had well pissed her off.
Then the car came into sight, and it honked. Someone
recognising him. He put his hand to his face, cupped
over his eyes, protecting the sun from them. The honk
again.

A knocking from behind him. Anton turned and
looked up to his bedroom window. Tim there, staring
out. Pointing. He thought he was trying to convey the
question of who it was. Anton shook his head and then
returned his look to the car.

Small thing. Red. It looked newish. Then he saw
the driver.

Sister Jean. He waved, and smiled. He *was* happy
to see her. Hadn't in some time as it happened. But
what could she be doing there?

She pulled the car around and over to the side of
mother's little run around. Jumped out. She looked
breezy and happy. Oh well. At least it should put a
smile on mum's face. She whipped her blond hair
around, out of her face, and hurried to Anton's waiting
arms, her face pushed into his chest. "Good morning."
She squeezed him, tightly. "Big brother," she
whispered.

"What are you doing here?" he asked. His hands
wrapped around her without the same vigour she used,
but his fingers knotted together behind her back
nonetheless, holding her in place. Tight against his

body.

"News," she said. "I have news."

Tim was rapping hard on the window now, trying to get attention of his own, and mother squealed as she burst from the front door. "What is it?" Anton asked.

"Later," she said, pulling away from him. She waved. Over to mum. Then went to her, the two of them in a hug.

Anton looked up to the window. Tim was gone. Probably looking for his trousers. He turned, ignored by his mother as she ushered Jean into the house. He could hear her gushing over his sister. So nice to have visitors. So nice to see her. He screwed his face up and wondered what the news was going to be.

———

Richard awoke. The sound of a car horn alerted him. He was too tired to care, and if he'd only just heard the sound of the car, him standing and shouting wasn't going to get heard, so he just sat there in the straw.

"You've given up," she said.

"I have not." He looked at her. She was starting to rot. Then he looked away. He didn't want to admit it, did he? He'd not been there long enough to give up, but he had, hadn't he? Fuck. Richard rolled around to his knees and faced the wall where the chain he was held with terminated. He rolled it around his wrist to anchor it and he pulled.

"Nice arse," she said.

Richard ignored her, grunting in anger and frustration and strain. He stopped. Air heaving in and out, tiring so quickly. "I can't," he said through the breaths.

"No," she said. "You're probably not the first one to be here, so why would it be easy for you to yank it off like that." She snorted. "If only you'd performed last night." He shot her a look, but she was gone.

"Yeah," he said. "You go and hide." He rolled his shoulders and drew a deep breath. Took the chain, and then let the air out. It was no use. If he was getting out of there, he was getting out another way.

C H A P T E R   1 5

Danny held Shirley's hand. He could see the spire of the church above the houses in the village. Finding it was going to be the easy part. His heart raced. He couldn't stop it. To be honest, he was scared. But he wasn't going to admit that to anyone.

Shirley squeezed his hand like she could hear his thoughts, so he squeezed it back.

"We'll find him," she said.

He nodded without a word.

To the left of them, they passed a typical cottage you would find on the cover of a home and garden magazine. White painted, thatched roof. Small windows with Georgian bar glass. The front door opened, and a small elderly woman stepped out. She had a cardigan on and was carrying a watering can. Danny stopped and for a split second, the two of them met eyes.

He sensed she felt something. Like she recognised him. Something close to a forgotten memory coming to the surface. He did look surprisingly like his brother. So perhaps—

Then she looked away and tottered slowly to the beds. Tipping the can up.

Nothing came out.

The two of them stood and watched her. A moment passed as she went from flower bed to flower bed tipping an empty watering can, miming this act, when a man followed her out. He hurried—albeit slowly to her side—and put his arm around her. He spoke quietly and restrained. "Come on Dolly," he said. "Let's get you back in the house." He took the can from her.

"I'm just watering the plants," she said.

"I know. Good job." He guided her around in a semi-circle, giving a quick glance to the two who stood there, staring. Shirley looked away, quickly. But Danny met his look. The old man looked tired.

Then he too looked away and pulled on Shirley's hand, taking her towards the church. "Damn," she muttered, "To be like that."

Danny nodded. *Yeah*. The two of them rounded the corner. The church, a way down the road. He could see that there was no bike there, but he could see the bollards that his brother would have used to chain his bike to. They circled an old phone box. As they got closer, Danny could see that there was still a phone in there. It'd been a while since he'd seen one of them. Most of the boxes–those that were left these days, stood empty, relics of the past.

"It's not here," she said.

Danny led her forward to the spot. He could see where Rob would have put it. In his mind's eye, he imagined the bike there. He looked closely at the ground like he might see a tire track or something. Shirley squeezed his hand and pulled him, knowing that there was no point in standing there wishing his bike was there. "We could ask in the church," she said. "Can't hurt, can it?"

Danny nodded, letting her drag him towards the open doors of the small church. The steeple, reaching up to God. They entered and the church smell invaded Danny's nose. It had been years since he'd been in a house of God. Didn't believe. Not anymore. And certainly not *now*. A glance at the bullshit paraphernalia on display. Flyers for the local bake sale. All that shit. Then they stepped deeper into the church.

There was a vicar standing at the front. Seemed to be busying himself with a rack of candles or something. Danny led the way, and Shirley hung back a little, subconsciously maybe.

The old man smiled. "What can I do for you, my children?" he asked, as Danny approached.

Danny told him he was looking for his brother, his bike parked out front some weeks back. Showed him the photo.

The old vicar looked dutifully at the picture, but told Danny he didn't recognise the man. "I do remember seeing a motorbike parked out there, though, for a few days."

"A few days?" Danny grunted. His eyebrows going up.

"Yes. Most unusual to see that sort of vehicle

here."

"Did it move in between?"

"Oh," he said, looking off into some middle distance. "I don't think so."

Danny nodded, resting his hand on the vicar's shoulder. "Thank you." He pulled a few notes from his wallet and pushed them into the donation box that hung from the wall before turning and picking Shirley up on the way out.

"Any use?" she asked.

"Old man says the bike was here for days. Barmaid said she only fucked him once." He shrugged it off. "I don't see the priest lying. But I don't think she was either." He glanced down at her.

"So, what was he doing the other few days?"

"That," he said, "is the question."

CHAPTER 16

Richard could see his breath in the air. The dip in temperature had been sudden. He wondered what the time was. It had been dark for a while, but not long enough for it to be approaching morning.

Although he might have blacked out.

It was hard to tell.

He reached up and felt the side of his face. The lump was going down. And he didn't feel sick. So maybe there were going to be no long-term side effects? He snorted out a pathetic half laugh. Long-term. Like anything was *long-term* now. He shivered in the night. One of the cows snorted.

He returned the snort, trying to see if he could communicate with the bovines.

It didn't snort back.

Just a coincidence then. Richard shook his head. Right. Okay. He could hear his own voice in his head, telling him to try to think straight. Hold it together. Stop trying to communicate with the cows in snorts. Teeth chattered and he clamped his mouth shut. Everything hurt. *Everything*. He heard a noise outside the barn. Probably the pigs. Then he saw Reggie, but she was just in his head. Curling into a ball, he sobbed. Knees tight on his chest, the tears rolled down his face. Blubbering out long, indecipherable moans.

Then a flash of light across the barn. Between the slats. He shut up. Held the cries in. There was someone out there. He breathed quickly, stopping the sobs. The light flashing around the floor. Then the barn walls.

Coming.

He curled tighter. What the fuck could they want now? Unless they were going to use this machine that they'd threatened? But why do that at this … *ungodly* hour. Everything they did was ungodly, wasn't it? He wasn't a believer, really. Never thought much about it to be honest, but he'd considered himself a good man, an honest one. Moral. He had no idea, really, what it meant to be Christian, but he felt that he could be considered Christian. That was one of the good guys, right? But these people were monsters.

The door to the barn cracked open and Richard could see nothing but more light. Someone is there. It flashed over onto him, blinding him. He cupped his hand on his face. "Who's there?" he asked quietly.

Like it was going to matter. It was either him or her. He was fucked either way. Literally. He broke a smile. Puns. Great. His brain was turning to mush. Clearly. "What do you want now?"

The light focussed on him for some time. Like he was being considered. Then the light—the person, presumably—came into the barn and the door closed.

Still blind by the darkness, Richard watched the beam of the torch bounce across the side of the barn. Out of sight, then back. Still curled into a ball. *What are they doing?* he wondered. Maybe it was the wife. That was it. She'd come back without the husband. See if she could get a better shot at laying him without the husband watching. He closed his eyes briefly, remembering what she looked like. She did technically have a better chance without the husband watching, but it still wasn't a good one. Slim to none. He couldn't shake the betrayal he'd be imposing on Reggie. Fucking someone else. That was the reason, stopping him more than anything else.

He rocked his head back. Who are you kidding? It was all of it. Everything was stopping him. Fucking rapist motherfuckers.

There was a rolling sound. Deep. A motor turning and then starting. A low rumble. Suddenly, lights came on around him. Blinded, now by the light, Richard blinked and squinted, trying to see as the brightness burned his eyes, watering, he tried to see through. The barn lit better than during the day. He could finally see all of it. And then she came from beside the stalls.

A young woman. One he hadn't seen before.

"Who … *Help me.*" He raised his hand in the chain. "Please."

She flicked off the torch she carried and looked at him without moving. Studying him clearly, like she had from the door, with the torch. Richard's heart sank. She was one of them, wasn't she? "Who are you?" he asked, relaxing back, the idea of rescue gone.

"Jean," she said. "And you?"

It was refreshing to be spoken to like a human being. "Richard," he replied.

"Mother's?" she asked.

Richard nodded. *I guess so.* "So, you're the daughter. I think I met—saw—your brothers. Couple of young guys came and gawped at me …" he let the sentence drop away, unsure in that moment if it was yesterday or the day before. Or even if yesterday was yesterday, depending on what time it was now.

Seeming to note the confusion, she asked, "You okay?"

Richard raised his eyes to her. "No, not really." He smirked. The humour of the situation overriding his hate and anger for just a moment. It gave him time to look at her. She was pretty. Blond. Young, like the boys. Late teens or early twenties, maybe. She was holding her hand to her face, a finger in her mouth like she was thinking. She slowly came to him. Closer, she put her boot—looked like riding boots—between his knees, forcing his legs open a little, and then pushing them apart.

Richard didn't stop her. He didn't see much point. It was apparent she was inspecting the stud for the family. And he didn't want another beating. Not just for insolence. She looked down between his legs.

"Nice," she said. "Does it get hard?"

Richard shook his head. "Not at the moment, no," he replied dryly. "It's broken."

She nodded. Hand dropped to her shirt, and she began to toy with the buttons. Like she was excited.

Fucking hell. Richard watched her. He was confused. She couldn't be thinking that. Not when he was there simply to impregnate the other woman. This woman's supposed mother. But he looked into her eyes and saw a look of … what was it? It wasn't lust. She wasn't desiring him. It was something else. She wanted him. Like when he was on a diet and he was standing outside the bakery, looking at the eclairs.

She crouched. Legs open. Splayed. "I want you to make me pregnant."

What?

As if she could hear his thoughts, she said, "I want you to fuck me. Is that so hard to believe?"

Richard looked down at himself. Emaciated. Weak. Broken. Bruised. Why did all these fucking weirdoes want to fuck him? Christ. "What?" he muttered finally. He looked back to her, and she had already started to take her shirt off.

Naked beneath. Her body, young and pert. Tight.

It still didn't move him, of course. "Why?"

"I want a kid," she said. "And you're virile, right?"

Richard shook his head. He barely knew what the word meant, let alone if he was or not. "You're all whack jobs." He closed his legs, hiding the goodies from the loon.

She pulled her shirt from herself, and dropped to her knees, crawling to him. Her fingers sliding in between his closed kneecaps where her boot had been before. Trying to cantilever his legs open. "Fuck off," he muttered.

He thought about attacking her. Punch her in her stupid face. Splatter her fucking blood everywhere. Tear her ugly cunt face off her skull and fucking eat it. But he breathed slowly and stopped himself. He'd just die for it, wouldn't he? They'd come in and find him there, with the corpse chained to the wall.

A spark of thought.

Richard wrangled the chain around between them. "You know what would help?" he asked.

She looked at the chain and then at him. There was little behind the eyes, like she was hyper focussed on one thing, and one thing alone. Her fingers were already around his flaccid penis and was inexperiencedly attempting to cajole an erection.

"Take these off and I'll make you a baby," he said. He tried his very best to sound sincere. Fuck it. If she did take them from him, he'd be so pleased, he might pop a chubby. He'd still grab the nearest thing and batter her with it. She was still toying with his junk, flopping around uselessly in her hand. She even dipped her head down and spat on it.

Gross.

Richard tried not to look like he might vomit at her touch. "Please," he said. "It'll help me …" he motioned to his cock with his eyes, "… you know." She had released his cock and stood, and for the briefest of seconds he thought she was going to get a key or something, but instead she was kicking off her boots and trying to shimmy out of the too tight jeans she wore.

Suddenly naked, she pushed herself on top of him, clumsily trying to achieve a cowgirl position, straddling across him, gyrating. "You like this?" she asked. Or said. It was hard to tell.

Pushed to his back and with her across him, he could see the appeal, in certain situations, just not this one. She wasn't and couldn't *do it* for him. He waved the chain at her. "This," he said. "Take this off, and I'll like it."

She huffed. Put her hands on his chest, and in one final attempt to not need to do that, she ground her vagina on to his penis. Richard could feel the warmth. It was the only attractive thing. Human warmth.

Then she grunted—annoyance—and pushed herself up away from him. She went over to the stalls and disappeared from sight. Richard wondered if she was going to get a pitchfork or something and run him through for being a cunt, or maybe get her father and tell him what an unreasonable arsehole he was being, or maybe—

She came back from the stall and was carrying the key. "You'd better get it up, right?" she asked.

Richard nodded, not being able to believe his luck. Maybe she was inbred or something? Something had to make her *this* stupid.

She crouched over him and started to fiddle with the clasp on his wrist.

Richard looked over at Reggie in the corner. She had her hand over her mouth in surprise. It was happening. It was really happening.

She dropped the clasp from his wrist, still straddled across him. The chain falling flaccid to the straw. "There," she said. "Now. Uppy-uppy."

Richard rubbed his wrist quickly, the feeling of something else there besides metal. Then he pulled his fist back and thwacked the bitch. He punched her harder than he'd ever punched anyone or anything in his life. Fucking hurt, too. Her head snapped back, and she grunted, falling away from his hips where she sat. Richard, frozen for just one second, then pushed himself to sit. Then up. He was free. He looked at her. She was bleeding from the face, pawing at herself. She even seemed stunned. "Stupid cunt," he said.

Richard ran to the door. His feet moving slower than he'd like. Stumbling as he tried to get blood flow. Weak without food.

"Fucker," she said.

Richard stopped at the side of the stall. Looked back. She was pushing herself to her feet. He glanced to the side. There was a motherfucking pitchfork. Right there. Speared into a bale of hay. He pulled it out and waved it at her like he was a gladiator in fucking 300. "You fucking inbred fucking cannibals," he said. He wasn't really thinking about the words. They just spewed out of his mouth, tinged with bile and hate.

"Cannibals?" she replied. Her face screwed up a little. She seemed oblivious to her impending skewering.

Then Richard charged at her. She screamed. He thrust, and she dived away into the straw. He missed. Almost colliding with the wall. His foot trampling the chain that lay on the floor, painfully. She was rolling away, fighting to stand. Her shrill screams filled the barn.

"Run, Richard," shouted Reggie.

Richard dropped the pitchfork and ran to the door. His ache to make her pay waned as he pushed the door open. The lights on the side of the house coming on, the yard flooding with yellow luminescence. He looked around wildly. The doors of the farmhouse bursting open. Lewis. Gun in hand. Behind him. Maisie.

She was screaming blue fucking death.

Lewis's gun went up. The air filled with the sound of gunfire, Richard barely finding the time to turn, let alone, disappear into the night.

He ran. The shot missed. He turned heel towards the darkness and sprinted. The pain of a thousand volts running up his feet with every step. So cold he could barely feel them, yet absolute stabbing with every foot into the mud. The dirt. The gravel. He ran to the first fence and hurled himself over. Into thick mud and muck, crashing to the shit on the other side.

Squealing.

Horrible screams from something inhuman. He rolled in the mud. A massive, fat, fucking pig running at him. Richard screamed out in fear. This monster coming at him. Mouth gorged open. Gnarled broken teeth dancing from the darkness. He scrabbled backwards, getting to his feet. A glance back. Lewis running towards him. The girl, naked at the door of the barn. Maisie. Richard threw himself across the pigsty, foot up into the fence and over. The other side, harder. His shoulder making a wild gristle sound as pain speared through him.

He pushed, desperate, back to his feet again. Pain ravaging his naked body. Hands shaking, his stomach turning like a tom bowler. Breath, struggling to reach his lungs, he forced himself away from the fence, towards the night. He was so hungry for the darkness, a yearn to vanish, he pushed forward.

Then the fire from the gun again.

A thousand needles poking into his shoulder. Buckshot. The force of the blast knocked him forward to his knees and over onto the dirt. He heard Lewis shout out in celebration that he'd *gotten the crit'er*.

Richard pushed back to his feet, into the shadows, running to the side of the barn. A look back, and Lewis was running now. Richard turned, charging into the blackness. Sudden pain. He fell. Crashing to the ground.

Lewis turned the corner. A torch up, he flashed it around. Richard saw the car he'd fallen over. Their car. Nestled in the dark behind the barn. His shins now bleeding as much as his shoulder. Behind it, a bike. Big thing. And beyond another car, and another. These fuckers had been doing this for *years*. He rolled to his knees. Crawled forward, trying to move on, making slow progress. Escape. The sound of footsteps on mud, squishing and sticking. He turned, looking back into the light from the house, the silhouette of the man hard against it. Torch up. "Mother fucker," he yelled. He came to Richard's side as he pitifully tried to push on. Booted him in the ribs as he crawled.

Richard rolled to the side against the car. Grunted out in pain.

"Takin' advan'age of my little girl," he muttered, a second boot going in.

He howled in pain, the buckshot wounds in his skin burning like fire, the boot kicks to the ribs feeling like he'd been shot again. He tried to move, but Lewis bent down, taking his ankle and dragging him uselessly back to the barn.

The girl there. "Mum, it's what I've been trying to say. I've decided to have a kid."

"You heathen lit'le slut." Maisie screamed the words into her face.

Richard watched, pulled along through the mud. The two women looking down on his naked body.

"But why?" Maisie continued. "Why him?"

"He's good stock. I heard you telling dad."

"But he's mine," Maisie continued. "Look at youse, youse could have any man you wanted."

The darkness of the barn covered Richard as he was dragged back inside. Bitter, and in pain, his chance gone. Lewis released his ankle, Richard groaning in pain. Lewis picked up the chain, giving a hiss sound, aggravation and anger that his little girl had done something so fucking stupid. Then he clamped it back on Richard.

Richard tried to stop him. Of course he did, but the pain in his shoulder was too much. Then as Lewis stood over him, he sneered, spitting in his face. "Piece of shit," he muttered. He went to the other side of the barn and placed the shotgun down, carefully and with reverence.

Then he returned to Richard, who was doing little more than cowering. "Please," he said. He wanted to tell Lewis that he'd have done the same thing, but he covered his face as Lewis bent over him throwing punch after punch into his body, until his hands moved from his face to protect that, and then Lewis's fists dropped there.

A darkness rose inside him. He wailed and cried, but his sounds got weaker as his breaths got shallower. Blood filled his nose, then his mouth. He rolled on the straw, turning. Spitting the fluids on to the ground. A jab to the side of the head. White noise filled both his eyes and his ears. He grunted, but didn't even hear it in his own head, full of whistles and thuds.

Blackness and darkness taking him, the pain lowering to dull thuds like he was being driven over, again and again.

Until the sweet warmth of nothing.

C H A P T E R   1 7

Cold and hurt, Richard wished he hadn't awoken. Not that morning. He hadn't slept. He was sure of that. He was just unconscious. He drew air in, tasting the acrid smell of pee in the air. He hadn't moved or felt around or anything like that. He was just lying there, one eye open in the barn. The taste of piss in the air. He looked up to the ceiling, afraid to move too much too quickly as he knew pain would ravage him hard.

Head thumping. Mouth dry. He was severely dehydrated. The taste of dried blood meeting the piss in his throat. He groaned, finally taking the chance and rolling onto his back. His body hurt. Torso. It felt like he'd been dropped off a cliff. Ribs screaming with each breath that was anything more than shallow. He touched himself. Gently. His torso, a mass of lumps and swellings, welts that weren't there before. He could feel the sobs coming from him, barely able to hear them, this interminable whistle in his eyes, filling his head. "Fuck," he whispered. It sounded like he was in a cave.

He could feel extra cold on his back. He was lying in wet. Must be his piss. Peed in his blacked-out state. He pushed himself around a little, finding little reason to get from the straw and cause himself any further discomfort than he was already in.

"You know that they're going to really fuck you up, now, don't you?"

Richard opened his eyes, Reggie stood over him. "I know." The words from his mouth dull and bassy.

"That was your only chance."

He also knew this, pointing out the obvious. He lay there, looking up at her. "I don't want to die here."

"I don't want you to, but what are you going to do?"

Richard pushed himself to his elbows. Looked down at his damp torso. Crawled from the piss spot and over to the other side. He checked himself over. No way of knowing if that fucker had broken any bones in the beating, but he wouldn't be surprised. It certainly hurt enough. He probed himself, prodding the swellings and bruising.

"Stop that," she said. "It won't help."

He gave her a quick look. Then around the barn. "What time is it?"

She shrugged. "Not a notion," she said. "Early." Reggie turned and looked at the light cracking through the walls. "Maybe," she added on.

Richard snorted, leaning back against the wall. "Fucked that up, didn't I?"

"Shouldn't have stuck around for her. Should have just run," she replied absently.

He looked down. His cock hanging flaccid between his legs. All because of that. His gaze turned up to Reggie. She was starting to look like a zombie. Flesh hanging from her, her eyes whiter than they should be. Skin pale. There were clumps of her hair missing. Richard closed his eyes and wished her away. He knew she wasn't there, really, and that made it worse, that his mind had pictured her like that, and not like she was. He let a blub escape his lips. Didn't mean to. It just crept up on him.

And when he opened his eyes, she was gone.

C   H   A   P   T   E   R   1   8

Danny pulled out of Shirley. She was shuddering, her orgasm still shaking her. He slipped down her and flicked his tongue over her clit. She moaned, getting louder, and then pushed her fist to her mouth, stifling the scream.

He could taste his semen. Pulled away from her, and gently bit her inner thigh. She shivered, whispering, *God.* Danny rolled over on the bed and crawled up next to her, pulling the sheet over their naked bodies. He looked across the room at the kettle and wished he had a cup of coffee, but wished he didn't have to go and make it.

Shirley dove herself in under his arm and he wrapped it around her. Squeezing her. "Wonderful," she said.

He felt like she was holding something back. Wanting to say something that she didn't, quiet. She'd been like this yesterday, too. It was one of the reasons he hadn't mentioned to her about his missing brother. It changed things. Of course it did. He'd become a man on a mission now, not just a biker running around the country getting into adventures and shit. He slipped his arm out and pushed himself from the bed, letting the covers drop over Shirley. Went and flicked the kettle on.

"Oh," she said. "Yes, please."

Danny nodded, turning the mugs over. Then he went to the toilet. Needed to pee. He sat on the seat and looked himself in the eyes in the mirror opposite. He had this sinking feeling now. Pretty much had since the vicar, the bike. There for days, now gone. A fart escaped him and he wished he'd closed the door properly, so he could cultivate it. Never mind. His eyes flicked across his own and he stood. Flushed. Shook his thoughts of his brother from his head, and returned to the bedroom, the kettle rolling and clicking off.

"What now?" she asked as he finished making the coffee.

"I want to grill the chick in the bar a little more."

"Think she knows more than she's letting on?"

He handed her the coffee. "I don't think so, not about that. But I don't get the impression she's exactly loyal to the area."

"I don't get you." She sipped the coffee.

Danny sighed, getting on the bed. "I don't think she's lying about it—spending the night with him, you know, but the way she talks. We've been to enough of these inbred little villages—the fucking Cotswolds— to know what people are like. She's banging any dick that comes her way. Doesn't seem like the type to be embroiled in some convoluted plot."

Shirley shook her head, pushing the covers under her arms. "He could have just left."

Danny shrugged. That was true. He *could* have. But it didn't feel right. She was game. He wasn't that hot. If this barmaid *had* fucked him, there was no way he would have gotten lucky enough in the intervening day to get lucky again. He probably wouldn't have left her bed until she made him. Christ. They'd still be banging now.

No. Something happened.

"I just want to ask her about the locals. The people that live around here. Anyone else he might have bumped into." He got back up off the bed.

"Now?" she asked. She looked at the time. "The pub won't be open yet."

Danny slumped back down. She was right. "I saw a tearoom near the church. It's probably shit, and all *stay off the moors*, but you wanna go for a scone for breakfast?"

———

Shirley had held his hand until they got back to the pub. When they entered and saw that the same woman was behind the bar, Danny let her go and without a word she slipped away, upstairs, to allow him to talk.

He went to the bar. She was sharp. She eyed him, carefully, but not obviously, as he approached and sat. He smiled at her, at her keenness. Something he wasn't expecting from a barmaid in an old, village pub. That might be an advantage.

"What can I do for you?" she asked. "Beer?"

The way she asked it, she knew he wasn't there for that. Well. Not only for that, at least. "Please," he said. "How are you today?"

She glanced to the door that led to the rooms upstairs like the question was loaded, or perhaps that Shirley might be waiting there to catch them up to no good. "Fine," she said, pulling a pint. "You?"

"Fine," he replied. She put the pint down and turned away, busying herself with glasses and such. Looking busier than she actually was. He tapped the rim of the glass, gently.

"What is it?" she asked, sensing he was trying to ask for more than a beer.

He smirked. She was probably used to being asked into a threesome or some shit. People passing through wanting more than the scenery on display. "My brother," he said.

She turned and looked, perhaps more comfortable that it wasn't going to be a question about her. "Yeah?"

"I spoke to the priest at the church," he watched her carefully trying to see if she gave anything away.

"Father Dowd. Nice man," she said, giving nothing away.

"I don't know, something about my brother leaving doesn't feel right. Do you think there is somewhere local he might have moved onto? Someone else?"

She looked down him and smiled. "Each to their own, but I don't get complaints. If he was planning on staying, I would have thought he would have at least made a play for me, you know." She looked down herself like, *you see this, right?*

Danny couldn't help but follow her look. Yeah. He did. And his brother would have, too. "Anywhere around here he might have found work?"

She shrugged, picked up a glass and started polishing it. "Plenty of farm work in these parts."

"Any weirdoes that might have picked a fight with him?"

She grinned. "Look, between you and me, most of this lot are weirdos. But picking a fight? That, I doubt. Mostly, they're a good bunch around here."

"Mostly?"

"There are families who are more unapproachable than others, but they've got farmland and have poachers and all sorts."

It sounded like she was making excuses to not badmouth the locals. "Hm," he grunted, taking a gulp of the beer. "Yeah."

"Look, I can't tell you what happened to your brother, but if you think he took work in the local area, which he may have, start with the farmhouses. They'll tell you if they've taken hands recently."

It was a place to start. Possibly, he supposed, that his lazy arse brother might have worked. *Possible.* It might explain the bike being moved. He shook his head, absently watching her as she got on with her work.

Lost in his own mind, however briefly.

CHAPTER   1 9

Anton shuffled uncomfortably into the kitchen chair, pushing himself back as hard as he could, wishing he was invisible.

"I will beat your arse." Maisie stamped over to the table like a petulant child. Her face screwed up like a bulldog.

Jean backed away, slipping around behind Anton's chair. "What?" she was saying.

Anton shook his head and raised his coffee to his lips, wishing it was something stronger. It was always like this when Jean and Tim were home. Everybody getting in everybody else's way. It was so much easier when it was just the three of them. And whoever they had in the barn, should that be of consequence. He smiled to himself, remembering that time Lewis had decided that he wanted his and bound up a woman in there to fuck later. Maisie had fed her into the combine while he was ploughing the fields. He snorted back a laugh and nodded his head.

"What's that?" Maisie interrupted his thoughts. She was scowling at him now.

"What?" he replied quietly, more unwilling to tell her that he was thinking about the woman, than not being part of this conversation. "Sorry," he muttered.

Maisie leaned forward, showing her bosom. Anton could not help but take a peek, soon averting his eyes.

"You can get your own," she hissed at her daughter. "You don't need mine."

"There's enough to go around," she said haughtily. "Besides, I don't see what's wrong with it."

Maisie screwed her hand into a fist and waved it at her. "It's fucking weird," she said. "I should just …" she paused for breath, possibly deciding on whether or not to beat Jean, when the door opened and Lewis came in.

He stopped and looked between the three of them and shook his head. "I don't know." He went to the sink and looked out to the warm orange of the sun as it tenderly stroked the farm to wake. "Anyways. He's still there. All snug."

"You didn't kill him, then?" Anton asked.

Lewis shot him a look. "I told you last night. I was too far away with the shotgun to do much damage, and I know how 'ard to beat a boy to tune him up without killin' him."

Anton's eyes hung heavy. This whole debacle had been going on pretty much the whole night.

"Where's your brother?" Lewis asked.

Anton shrugged. "Bed? Where I should be."

Lewis shook his head. "I don't think so farmer man. You need to be out working even if you've been up all night. Think of the times you'll have to be up calfing."

"Calfing," he repeated. Probably wasn't even a word. "Yes."

"It's the life you chose," he continued, wiping his hands dry on the tea towel. He stopped. Realised Maisie and Jean were both staring at him. He looked at the towel and thought it must have been that. "Sorry," he muttered, tossing it to the side. Neither of them acknowledging his gesture, he shrugged. "What?"

"Where do you stand on this, Dad?" Jean crossed her hands over her chest.

Oh, God. "Well," he said, looking around the room for an escape. Trying to buy time. Trying to think fast. "I … I …" he certainly didn't want to upset his daughter, Heaven no. He glanced at Maisie. She'd also crossed her arms. There was no right answer here. He supposed deep down, he would prefer it if Jean had her own bloodline, for several reasons. But he couldn't say that. He could see the hope in her eyes as she waited for him to take her side. But looking at Maisie, he couldn't do that either. "No, well." He looked at Anton. "Come on, boy. I need to show youse something."

The room drowned in silence as the two men left, Jean and Maisie staring at each other in silence.

"So, what are you going to do?" Maisie asked.

Jean huffed. "I guess I'll have to find another

man's batter then, won't I?"

Maisie was nodding slowly. "Yes. Besides. That young man out there will 'ave to start performing today." She turned and looked out the window. "One way or the other."

———

Tim stood in the bedroom. Naked from the waist down, watching through the window. He could feel his excitement rolling about inside of him. Always the same first thing in the morning. Stood at the window, he watched Anton and Dad. The two of them stood with the pigs. Dad had a foot up on the fence, arm rested across his knee. He was probably imparting great wisdom to Anton about running the place. Tim shook his head. It wasn't fair that Anton got the whole farm. They should all share it. He cupped his testicles and squeezed slightly. "Share and share alike," he muttered to himself.

C H A P T E R   2 0

Richard lay on the straw. The fucking stuff pricked him. Teasing his sore flesh with sharp jabby points. He turned, everything flaring in pain as he did. The burning of the beating. His shoulder, full of buckshot, he was sure. When he looked at the straw in the light, he could see the blackened blood as it had dried to everything. All of it. He could hear voices. Men talking. It was strange though, like there was the sound of running water the whole time as well.

He curled his legs under him. A little warmer now than last night. He could feel Reggie looking at him. "I tried," he whispered.

"Yeah, you did."

He glanced up to her. She was standing at the wall of the barn, turning, she looked out through one of the cracks. "What do you see?" he asked.

"A couple of them talking."

Nothing he didn't already know. There was another voice. Higher pitched. A woman, perhaps.

Reggie looked back the other way. "A woman." She turned to face him. Her skin, a dull grey. Gashes in the flesh where she was breaking away. Rotting. Dirty. She strolled to him, her stank filling the space between them, and he shook it away.

"I don't know what to do now," he said, looking away like she was really there.

"They'll put you on the machine."

"I know."

"Probably today."

"I know."

His attention was taken by the cows in the stalls moving. He glanced over, jarred in surprise, slightly, then back, and she was gone. "Damn it, Reg," he whispered. "I wish you were here."

The barn doors opened and the sun crashed into the darkness. Richard cowered away from it, like it burned as if he were a vampire. "Please don't," he whimpered even before his eyes had gotten used to the light and he saw who was coming in.

Maisie strode into the shadows to the side of the door, and the voice, coming from a silhouette, Lewis, "You really want this one?" he said. Even Richard heard the disdain coming from him.

"Yes," she said, quietly. "My eggs are ready."

Richard felt his stomach turn. Jesus Christ. The shadow that was Lewis moved, and behind him another. And another. Three of them with her. Must be all the boys. "How can you do this, you fucking *bitch*?" he shouted, spitting the words at Lewis, not Maisie. "Letting your wife fuck other men?"

"Let'ing," he chuckled. "And way gone are the times you can talk about fucking. That's gone now. Now we're doin' it the … *easy* way."

"Easy way," muttered Richard.

"Well, it don't need to be 'ard, does it?" Lewis went out of sight, around the corner of the stalls into the darkness, unseen. Anton and Tim stood in the doorway of the barn, watching, like *muscle* in a Jason Statham film, glowering in the corner until they were needed. Maisie, there in the shadows, waiting.

Richard focussed his attention on her. He needed her to be on Team Richard. That was all. "I can do it," he said. "I want to." He smiled at the woman cast in shade. Not able to make out her features. "It'll be so much nicer." Even he heard the crack of desperation in his voice.

"For youse maybe," she snorted.

Richard's heart sank. This was it. They were going to do whatever it was that they were going to do *now*.

Lewis reappeared with a trolley, pushing it clumsily through the straw into the opening between him and Richard. The two younger men watching, leering. He could see their mirth. Richard pulled pathetically on the chain. He knew he couldn't get free, but he also wanted to try, damn it.

The trolley, closer, and Lewis moving things about on it, Richard could see, it looked like a hostess trolley, wheels and shelves. He looked at the items on it. It was set up like a home-made surgical table. Implements and instruments all laid out to be used on the top, and a motor, grimy and dirty on the bottom, and the doctor there, making sure everything was in its place, and everything had a place. He sighed, deeply, his eyes darting between them all. He really didn't see any point in begging.

Then Lewis said, "Take 'im."

The two younger men came forward, one on each side of Richard, in a pincer movement. He pushed himself weakly to his feet, the only option left to fight them off. He looked to each of them as they rounded and got closer to him. Then, at the same time, they pounced. One on each arm, as Richard pulled and struggled, his freedom taken instantly.

Between the dehydration and starvation,—and the fear—he never stood a chance. The two men held him, naked, stood, arms out to the side in some wretched Jesus pose, as Lewis took the thing from the top of the trolley. He came at Richard. This cylinder thing, looked like some cross between a sex toy and cow milker attachment. A belt to go around Richard, and a tube that came from the end. An electrical wire wrapped around the tube going to the motor.

"Hold him still boys," said Lewis.

Richard pulled his left arm, hard, trying to free himself by catching Anton off guard, but he failed, the young man's grip held firm. Then the right, but it was too late to have any surprise by then. He brought his foot up to try and kick at Lewis, but he was too weak and Lewis too quick. The man sidestepped his pathetic attempt at attack and continued to his body. He took Richard's cock in his hand and stuffed it roughly into the cylinder. Reaching around behind him and buckling the straps to hold it there. Richard pulled, pushed. Left and right, but the thing was held firm. Lewis backed up as Richard looked down at himself. This *thing* strapped to him. This milking machine.

"Down," Lewis said.

The two of them held Richard, then forced him forward and down, pushing him to his knees and then bending him forward, pushing his arse up into the air, downward dog style. "No," Richard … barked. "What are you doing?"

He got a mouthful of straw for his effort before twisting his face and watching Lewis. One of them had a hand on the back of his head, holding him with some ease to the straw. Lewis got something. It looked similar to the thing they had just strapped to him, but for the electrical cable coming out of the other end. Lewis went around to his side and Richard lost sight of him. One of the boys laughed.

Then Lewis stuffed the thing up Richard.

Richard grunted in pain, gritting his teeth, not wanting to give the bastards the pleasure of him crying out. He could take the pain and discomfort of this *thing* being stuck up his arse. He tried to relax, teeth grinding, his head thumping. Pain rolled over his lower torso as Lewis seemed to take glee in jamming it in there *real* good. Fucking Yorkshire hillbillies. Then Lewis came back into sight, and he went to the machine. Richard tried to move again, this overwhelming pain and his feeling of shame overriding all others. He was held fast.

Lewis dropped to a crouch and smiled at him. "Now youse be a good boy, yes?" His grin widened and he stood, turning to the machine. He poked and prodded it for a second or two, during which Richard struggled, as hard as he could to free himself. But they'd worn him down. Over the last couple of days … it was all part of the plan, clearly. He was being ground down to make this … easier. Then Lewis flipped the power on the machine.

The motor roared awake, and instantly the thing in his arse moved. It jerked and bounced and felt like it was going to rip him open and tear his flesh. He screamed, pain rolling through him.

Lewis shouted over the motor, "It won't take a second." Then he turned his attention back to the machine.

The pain as the thing in him vibrated and heaved back and forth as this shitty homemade dildo attached to a tractor motor ran. And then the other side moved. A suction suddenly pulling his cock, then releasing it. A wank motion.

"No," Richard cried out. He tried to move, but the two of them held him down firmly, clearly used to this sort of fightback. He yowled out in pain, yes, but also the heat of embarrassment overcoming him. The anger. They were raping him and there was nothing he could do. His head, pushed down harder into the straw, the straw filling his mouth as whichever of them it was, held him there.

Being milked.

C H A P T E R   2 1

Daisy stood in the corner of the pen. She liked when the master came and cleaned her pigsty out. He was shovelling some of the weightier shit to a barrow and he would remove it. She watched as he stopped and looked into the shit. Bent forward and probed it with his fingers. Silly master. That was shit. No need to put your fingers in it. She looked around him, the gate to the pen open. The draw of the open gate was strong. But she knew better than to try and get out to freedom. He was angry the last time she'd tried, and he'd beaten her. She'd made it to the barn where the fresh flesh came from before he'd tackled her to the ground and pushed her over. He'd picked her up in his muscular arms and carried her back.

Then he'd beaten her.

That was the last, and only time she'd tried to get free.

She glanced across to her brother. He was eyeing freedom, too. She hoped he didn't try to break free. He wasn't clever. He certainly wouldn't be able to get any further than she had.

Then the master took the barrow to the gate, and

out, closing it behind him. He wheeled it to the side of the barn, leaving it there and heading towards the house.

Daisy fatly plodded to the gate, the temptation to flee taken, and she watched him go into the house.

———

Lewis sighed and opened the front door, a quick look back to the pen. He shook his head. He went to the kitchen and stood, hands under the running water in the sink, while he watched out into the yard, absently. He was trying to keep his thoughts in check. He didn't need to have *thoughts*. He wiped his hands on the tea towel, leaving a skid mark of pig shit on it, before heading up the narrow stairs of the farmhouse. He pushed the bedroom door open.

Maisie was on the bed. She had the phial of the stud's semen in one hand and a teaspoon in the other. Carefully pouring some of the seed onto the spoon.

"That gonna work, is it?" Lewis asked. He turned to the bedside dresser and pulled it open. Pushed his fingers into the underwear and started rooting about for clean socks.

"Worked with Anton, din'it?" she replied.

Lewis glanced over his shoulder to see the spoon being inserted into her vagina. She tipped it, and then stirred like it was a really good cup of tea. Her look moved from the spoon to her husband, staring. "Perver'," she said, grinning. "Wanna cream pie?"

Lewis grinned but shook his head. "I don't think so. I'm worried about Daisy."

"What's the matter with 'er?" Maisie asked as she poured another spoon.

Lewis dropped his arse down on the edge of the bed. "She's still not chewin' up the teeth proper."

"I told you before, I don't think she can."

Lewis shot her a look. That didn't seem right. Surely pigs can chew teeth. They can chew bone. Can't they? He shook his head. "Yeah," he said, quietly.

"And that's the lot," she said.

He looked back at her. "All done?"

"Yes indeed. 'E didn't produce that much, did 'e?"

Lewis shook his head. "We can do it again la'er if youse think 'e's worth it."

She rolled onto her back and pushed her legs up the wall, aiding the semen's journey in the right direction. "I don't know," she said. "I thought 'e was going to be something 'e wasn't. Smart, he is. One of those learn'd types. Thinkin' all the time. Could be a good thing for the next one to be a learner."

"Like Tim you mean," Lewis said absently.

"Like Tim." Maisie glanced at him. "What do you think about Jean and this 'ere 'er wanting to procreate all of a sudden?"

Lewis shook his head. "She's grown up, ain't she? Wants a family of 'er own."

"Yeah, but why did she think she needed to come down 'ere and get my stud?"

Lewis shrugged. "That, I don't know, my lovely."

C H A P T E R   2 2

The engine on the bike didn't sound quite right to Danny. He'd been listening to it half-heartedly over the last few miles. He was concerned that he hadn't been taking care of her properly. He shook his head under the helmet and felt Shirley cling on tighter to him as they banked into the corner.

He slowed as they passed the turning into one of the farms. Over to a passing spot on the lane and he stopped. Pulling up and watching over to the fields beyond. The entrance to the farm was like a road in itself. A narrow drive of a couple of hundred yards before opening out to a farmyard.

Shirley tapped her helmet against his. "What do you think?" she asked over the motor's roar.

He could see farm buildings and such in the distance. Could be that they'd take helpers? He didn't really know what he was looking for. He shrugged. "Go and ask, I suppose." He kicked the bike back into gear and turned it around, back to the entrance and down.

———

Jean pushed her arse out as she pulled Tim's cock into her mouth. She took it deeply to her throat, licking the shaft. Pleasure tingled its way up her as Anton's cock delved into her, spreading her, his hardness, his cock … engorged. He was big at the best of times, but on this particular day, he'd outdone himself.

Perhaps because she had insisted the two of them go bareback for the first time.

Tim grunted, his pelvis moving in time with her suckling. As he fucked her mouth, Anton found the same rhythm, as the two of them fucked her. Her pleasure pushed to the edge as she felt her orgasm rise up and flood over her, but she didn't stop. She kept the two of them going, and feeling Tim rise towards completion, she pulled him from her mouth, giving him a little slap, his pre-cum flicking over her face. "Naughty, naughty," she said. He knew that wasn't allowed.

She clenched her glutes, sucking Anton into her further, tighter, and he started to fuck her harder. She could sense he was getting close to the edge. "Fuck, yes," she said. Pushing against him. Willing him to make her pregnant. She looked at Tim, still on his knees in front of her, edging himself with his fist. "Hold on baby," she said. "You're next."

She felt Anton come hard inside her and she waited for him to finish his strokes, before crawling forward and turning. Laying on her back and spreading her legs, presenting her creamy cunt to her other brother. "Fuck me good," she said.

Tim dropped down on her and slipped with ease into her, aided by Anton's sticky wet. He pushed into her tight warmth, his orgasm rising instantly. He jerked and she laughed as he came. Shuddering his pleasure out into her, mixing with his brothers.

"Wait," she said, quietly. "Listen."

She turned her head to the side, out of the way of Anton's waning cock, drooping over her face, semen bulbed from the end of it. She could hear something coming. A motorbike, maybe. She drew air in. "A biker," she said. She pulled herself from Tim and pushed Anton out of the way, hurrying naked to the window and looking out to see a motorbike coming down towards the farm.

"They'll see you," Tim said, rolling onto his back. He looked at Anton's cock. The bulb.

"Maybe they should." Jean started picking up her clothes, strewn to the bedroom floor, and pulling them on, dressing quickly.

Hurrying to the door, she was gone.

Tim looked up, to Anton's face, the two of them meeting eyes. "Need a hand?" he asked.

———

Danny pulled the bike to a stop just outside the gate into the yard of the farm. He sat there for a moment, giving Shirley no indication that she should move. Assessing the house, and the surrounding buildings. Looming around the back of the house, he could see outbuildings. Barns. That sort of thing. A couple of cars in the yard. He tapped Shirley's leg, and she swung herself off the bike.

Then he got off next to her. The two of them stood there, crash helmets on, watching the farmhouse.

The door to the building opened. A man. He was middle aged, and looked leathery and worn, and without question, was the farmer. Danny took his helmet off. He walked slowly through the gateway into the yard, not knowing what the protocol was with these places—some of them had fences and gates and some didn't. No one had seemed perturbed by him entering their land, but he was getting annoyed.

He was getting nowhere.

As the farmer crossed to Danny, he brought his hand up and waved. "'Ello," he called. Approaching, the two men got close. "Nice bike, that one."

Danny nodded, a smile accepting the compliment. "I was wondering if you could help me?"

"What can I do for you?"

Danny notcd that the man looked over his shoulder to Shirley, and there was a look of suspicion there. Danny glanced back; she hadn't taken her helmet off. Perhaps that was why. He pushed his hand into his pocket and pulled the photo of his brother. "I'm looking for this guy," he said, "I wonder, do you have workers or whatnot that stay here? Have you seen him?" He passed the picture to the man who looked into it, his nose screwed up.

"We don't usually take 'ands 'ere—I have my two

boys." He snorted up a loogie.

Danny's attention was drawn by the door to the farmhouse opening again and a young woman coming out. She was half dressed, pulling clothes on as she came. She was pretty. No more than twenty or so. Hurrying out into the yard even though she didn't have anything on her feet. She looked like she'd just got out of bed.

"Who's this?" she all but shouted as she crossed the yard.

The man looked back at her. He half passed the photo back to Danny. "This gentleman is looking for this other gentleman. Why don't youse go back in the 'ouse?"

She arrived at the two men and stood there, looking into Danny's face like a puppy. He looked away, disconcerted. Back to the man. "Well?" he said, perhaps a little too impatiently.

The man shook his head. "No, I've not seen him."

Danny thrust the photo towards the woman. "How about you?"

But the man stopped him, blocking the photo as he pushed it across. "She's only been here a day or so, so she hasn't either." The two men locked eyes for a moment, and then Danny raised his eyebrows.

"Thanks," he said dryly. He glanced at the woman. Back to the man. Something was wrong. Maybe it was that old adage of the farmer's daughters. Danny's eyes returned to the woman. She was certainly looking at him like he was the last hotdog in the shop window, and she hadn't eaten for a week. Could be that.

Could be.

He nodded his farewell to the two of them, returning the woman's look with a cheeky smile, intending to do nothing more than aggravate the farmer. Then he turned back to his bike. He could feel the two of them, their looks burning into his back. Watched Shirley as she too looked at them, through the slit in her helmet.

He got to the bike and put his helmet back on.

"What is it?" she asked.

"We're leaving," he said. A look back to the two people. Still watching. The two of them got on the bike and he started the engine, pulling the bike around and back towards the road.

Something was very wrong there.

———

Tim wiped his mouth with the back of his hand, and grinned at Anton, who stood at the window. "What is it?"

"I don't know," he replied, "but dad looks pissed."

Tim rolled onto his back and looked at the ceiling. Listened to the crows on the roof. The scuttle of their claws as they moved. "Come back to bed."

C H A P T E R   2 3

Richard curled into a ball, shivering. There didn't seem to be an inch of him that didn't burn. Not a single inch. The light between the cracks in the barn was lowering, and the sun was going down. Sniffing up snot into his throat, he swallowed it back, happy to have the liquid, even if it did raise a sickness in him. He shuddered, listening to the stomp of the cows in the … fuck it. He didn't even know what the cows looked like, let alone what they stood in. He opened his eyes and blinked away the pain in his forehead. Dehydration, probably. The straw. That was probably what they stood in.

He looked over to the machine.

They'd left it there to taunt him. It was far out of his reach, of course, otherwise he would have used every ounce of his strength to destroy it. But they knew that. He wrapped his fingers around the straw beneath him, blackened with his own blood. Some of it had come from his arsehole. He knew that. Some his nose and his mouth from where they beat him … after.

He wondered, briefly, what sort of internal damage they had done, and how long it was going to be before they killed him now. Now that they'd taken his seed.

He choked, his throat fiery like he'd swallowed glass. "Fuck," he muttered. He reached down and felt his cock and balls, cupping them. Sore. Like he'd been kicked over and over. They hadn't stopped when he'd finished, running the machine continually until he had come a second time, and then the beating started—but even then, they never turned any of it off. Letting the thing fuck him and suck him all the while the two young men kicked him and punched him and laughed at his pathetic attempts to protect himself. Maisie, watching the whole time. Smiling, getting off on it, probably.

"Don't stick your fingers around the back, will you?" Reggie's voice cut through the evening quiet.

"Why?"

"Wrecked," she said. She rounded the barn from behind him. "Gape."

Richard sobbed, his mouth hung open, dry and chapped.

"They'll kill you soon."

"Soon enough," he nodded.

"No way out."

"No way out." He looked at her. Rotten, the flesh blackening in the wounds. The blood the only colour on her apart from the dark green spider veins that slipped up and down her flesh.

"Given up."

His eyes met hers, milky white and dead. "Never," he said weakly. He was lying to himself of course. He knew that it was hopeless, and while he wasn't about to say he'd given up, it was most certainly … hopeless. And that was the same thing, right?

"Hope comes back," she whispered.

He looked to her, but she was gone. "Yeah," he said, rocking back to his arse, then regretting it, and flopping onto his side, into the straw, quiet. Listening for something that might give him hope.

That was when sleep took him. Beaten and exhausted.

———

A snap. Richard opened his eyes because something inside him told him to. He heard something. He was sure of it. Something outside the barn. He squinted into the blackness. No idea of the time. Hours since he last had his eyes open, of that much he was sure. He went to call out, then the memory of the girl coming to him to fuck presented itself, and he stopped himself.

He all but held his breath.

Watching the sparks of light caused by the moon dance and move. There was something outside the barn. Some … *one.* He watched, waiting to see if it was her. Whoever it was, was moving slowly. It could have been her. They came to the barn door. Paused. Then moved on. Shit. What should he do?

The figure moved towards the houses.

"Hello?" he said. The word came out quieter than he would have liked. Shit. "Hello?" he tried again, louder. The figure stopped. There was a pause that seemed to last forever, before whoever it was turned back and came to the side of the barn.

Richard could tell by the way the figure moved, it wasn't one of the family, besides, it wasn't using a torch, That was some indication. The figure just stopped at the barn and waited like they weren't sure they had heard the noise.

"Hello?" Richard hissed. "In here. *Help me.*" And there it was. That sudden spark of … hope.

The figure moved to the door of the barn, opening it slowly, carefully, *quietly.* He watched as the figure moved into the barn. Still cast in shadow, Richard couldn't tell who it was. But now in the barn, he could tell it was a man. He came over.

A biker.

The guy was dressed in a leather jacket and jeans.

Richard almost peed himself, overcome with something. The man, half visible, looked down on him.

"What the fuck?" he muttered.

"Help me out of the chain, please," Richard hissed quietly. "*Please.*" The second time he said it, it seemed to get the man into action. He dropped down next to him. Picked up the chain and followed it to the wall. "That's no good," Richard continued, "there's a key behind the stalls somewhere." He pointed and the man nodded, hurrying over to the barn and around, out of sight.

Richard's head spun. He felt so sick, but there was

a sudden urgency in him, one that wasn't there before. A newness. He waited for what felt like an interminable length of time. Listening. He could still hear the man there. Praying he wasn't going to leave.

Praying he was real and not some figment of his addled mind.

The cows shuffling about, the stranger so close to them. The silence cut as one bellowed out, causing a ripple of sound across however many of them there where. Cow after cow. He closed his eyes for a moment. The stranger had to be real if the cows could see him. He hissed, "Found it?"

Then the stranger re-appeared. He hurried over. Crouched, taking the lock from Richard's wrist. "What the fuck have they done to you?"

Richard shook his head. "They killed my wife."

The chain dropped off and the stranger helped Richard to his feet. With Richard's arm over his shoulder, the man took his weight in strong arms. "Come on."

The two of them returned to the door of the barn and out, to the left, moving closer to the house, before turning down the side of the barn and towards the edge of the property. They moved in silence for a while. Until they cleared the barn and were farther from the house.

Richard could barely move his legs, but he made himself. He dug in. Found the strength to help himself get far away from that barn. He was going to get to the police. He was going to make them pay. The stones on the ground dug into his flesh and he could feel the blood coming from him. The stinging of the dirt as it dug into the slits in his skin, ignored. He shook it away, taking as much of his own weight as he could.

The man led him to the trees and into the copse. It was harder to walk in there, but he did. Sticks and branches stabbing into him. The freedom pushing him forward. "Richard," he said. "My name is Richard. My wife, Reggie."

"Danny," the man replied. "Come on. Let's get you out of here."

The two of them came to a road.

A motorcycle ridden up and parked in the bushes. "You ride pillion?" Danny asked.

"I'll ride anything to get away from here," Richard said, sad. Danny got on and Richard, naked, sat behind Danny. Danny handed the man his helmet, and smiled, weakly at him. He took it and put it on. The two of them riding off. Towards the village. Richard held tightly to Danny. The vibrations of the bike pushing pain around his body, hard and fast. He wept, in the helmet. He wept for himself and for Reggie.

She was gone now. He knew that. He wasn't going to see her again.

C H A P T E R   2 4

Tim looked at the clock. It was nearly ten. He just wanted to go to bed but his father wasn't about to let it go.

"I just don't see why," he said. He looked at Maisie. She shook her head in agreement.

Tim noted that she had her hand resting over her belly like she was preggo. He shook the thought away. She was always the same when she was trying to conceive. He thought about Jamie, their youngest sister, away at school. She was in France on a trip at the moment.

Lewis leant forward and rested one hand on the table and the other in a fist, single finger out, pointing. He was looking at Jean but pointing at Anton. "These two, though?" The point went around the table a little to himself.

"They're good people. I'll have a fine child."

He shook his head.

"It's not like *you* want me anymore," Jean blurted. The pout came out. Then she folded her arms over her chest and slumped back in the chair. "You're unbelievable, you are." She huffed.

Tim tried to look away. It was a train wreck. Hard to look away from, but you had the feeling that someone was likely to die from it, and so you wanted to stare.

"How dare youse talk to your father like tha'," barked Maisie. She reached forward over the table and rested her hand on Jean's shoulder. "You know he still loves youse and wants youse in every way, but he's not get'in' any younger."

Lewis snorted and Maisie shot him a death stare.

"Anyway," Anton interrupted. "Any chance I could hit the sack?" He nodded up to the clock. "Getting late."

Lewis turned his attention to him, then. "You stay where youse are for now. Just because I ain't spoken to youse yet, don't mean I ain't got somethin' to say."

Anton slumped. Tim kept watching. That probably meant that Lewis had something to say to him, too. Fuck. He glanced at Jean, and Lewis cleared his throat, pulling his attention back to him. He had that look of *don't you be looking at your sister like that, young man*. He shrugged and looked away. It wasn't like her panties weren't already swimming in his and Anton's gravy. Actually, he was beginning to wonder what the point of any of this was. "Can't we just go out and grab someone for her? Like we do her?" The second her was joined with him pointing at his mother.

"Who's 'er, the cat's mother?" his father snapped.

"*Mother*," Tim corrected. "We can go along to

Snodmarsh or somewhere and grab one of the tourists. There is always tourists there."

"I don't want no tourist from Snodmarsh," Jean whined.

"You don't 'ave to 'ave a tourist from Snodmarsh," Maisie cried.

"Jesus Christ." Lewis held his head in his hands. Family. "Anton's right," he said quietly. "Let's all talk about it in the morning."

Shirley was tucking Richard into their bed. She glanced to Danny, who was watching from the door, then flicked her head to the bathroom, where the two of them headed, closing the door quietly behind them. "What the fuck?" she hissed. Danny had arrived less than thirty minutes before, this naked man with him, half unconscious. He'd managed to get him into the room without being seen—the man muttering something about Reggie and the police.

"I don't know," Danny said. "But I'm going to find out."

She looked him down exasperated. "You need to call the police, is what you need."

He shuffled to the left, and she could see he wasn't to be argued with. He was so angry he could barely control it.

"Your brother," she said, quietly. "You think he was there?" His eyes flashed when she asked. The answer a yes. "The police?"

He half shook his head. A snap to the side. "No. If he *was* there, I want answers from the people that live there. Richard says they killed his wife. I want to know if they had him. If they …" he let the words hang there. "I want to know."

Shirley nodded. "Then I'm coming, too."

He stared at her, looking like he was going to argue, before he seemed to back down in his own head. Good. She was in no mood to be argued with. "What about him?" he asked.

Shirley looked through the crack in the door. "He's not going to wake for hours. He's broken. Bruised. We'll let him sleep and then call the police in the morning."

Danny drew air in. "Come on then."

———

Danny pulled the bike up to the bushes somewhere close to where he'd left it last time. Hard to tell how close, in the dark. Now it was fully pitch-black. The countryside unlit apart from the small amount of light being given off by the farm buildings. The two of them got off the bike, hanging their helmets over the handlebars. "Are you sure you want to do this? We get caught and there will be no end to the trouble."

Shirley nodded. "Of course."

The two of them ducked into the trees and disappeared. The darkness making it difficult to navigate. It didn't look the same as when Danny had brought Richard out, but he could see the lights of the farm disappearing and reappearing behind the undergrowth as they got closer. He crouched as they reached the tree line and pointed, as Shirley came down with him. "That barn there," he said. "I found Richard in it. Farmhouse to the left."

"What's to the right? I don't want to run into farmhands or anything if they have other buildings." She glanced to him, watching her.

"Good idea, but he said there were no hands. And I doubt they'd want members of the public hanging around if they were keeping people locked in the barn."

"I can't imagine what the fucking point could be."

Danny looked away from Shirley. He'd heard what Richard had said between the ramblings of a madman as they made their way back. A milking machine. Inbred monsters. Insemination. He didn't think it was a necessity to share that with Shirley. There was five of them. Three men. Two women. That was all that mattered. "I didn't check out the right. Didn't get a chance. I did see a whole bunch of buildings. I suppose …" he rubbed his chin. "There could be other people there. Other captives."

"You think?"

"Come on." He pushed himself back to stand and went through the shadows to the side of the barn. Heard movement coming from inside. "Cows," he hissed to Shirley. Then made his way to the far end of the barn, looking quickly around the corner. His eyes widening. "What the fuck?"

Shirley came up to his side and looked.

A car graveyard.

C H A P T E R   2 5

Danny's heart sunk. There had to be fifteen, twenty cars, maybe more, to the side of the barn. There were some that looked like they'd been there for months. Others … years. He walked to the first vehicle and ran his fingers over it. The plates showed it was nearly thirty years old, and it didn't look like it had moved much in the last twenty. He moved quietly between the cars, the sounds of animals raising and falling as ambient sound in the darkness. The closer he got to the front, the newer the vehicles seemed to be. Mostly cars, varying from hatchbacks to sedans. Mostly low to mid-range. Nothing expensive. He could feel the hate and anger rising in him as his cogs turned and scenarios changed. Nothing rich and expensive. Nothing from someone that might be missed. No one on a work route or a family on holiday.

People that disappear.

He reached the front. There was a car there that could have only been there a few days. Had to be Richard's and … what did he say his wife's name was? He shook his head, squinting at the motorbike leaning up behind it. Tears welling in his eyes. Shirley saw. She put her hand on his arm, tender, a quick feeling passing between them. "Call the police," she whispered.

He could hear the fear in her voice. Fear of what he might do.

But he shook his head. "No," he replied quietly. "They can come tomorrow." He pulled his arm, gently, from hers. He wasn't angry with her and didn't want her to feel that way. Over the last few days, he'd found her to be supportive, and necessary. He was starting to feel something for her, beyond the company and the fucking.

He shook his head, clearing his thoughts. "You can wait with the bike, if you prefer." He gave her a genuine look of concern, and a small smile.

"Like fuck am I missing out on the vengeance part of this. We're the next best love story in Britain. Can't miss out on the murder."

Danny smiled. Wry. He led the two of them making their way to the edge of the barn. He looked out to the other buildings shadowed in the night. There was no indication that anyone was anywhere other than the house. He kept low and the two of them made their way across to the outbuildings. After pausing to listen, the pigs snorting and in the distance a cow bellowing, he opened the door. A small building first. He stuck his head in and looked. A shed. Wide and open. He nodded to himself and went in. Scoured the shelves around the walls looking for something.

Nothing of use. Shirley stood at the door waiting for him. He shrugged and returned, moving on to the next one.

This building was taller. Wide doored. He pushed it open, a tractor in the middle of it. He went in, ignoring the big machine and around the edges. He grunted some satisfaction when he found what he was looking for.

A length of rope. Good. He pulled it over his shoulder and continued, picking up a pitchfork and looking at it, discarding it to the hay bales. Stopping, he glanced back to Shirley. She was standing at the door wielding an axe. *Yes*. That was perfect. He strode to her, kissing her deeply like he was the hero in an old black and white film and that he might call her *Dame* at any moment.

He took the axe from her, and she glanced around, bending and retrieving a knife from a low shelf. Long thing. Looked halfway between a kitchen knife and a machete. He was glad he'd bought her. She was good at this. He grinned. The two of them went across the open farmyard and to the door of the house.

———

Daisy watched the interlopers as they made their way to the master's house. She didn't know who they were, but it was very exciting.

———

Danny stopped at the door and waited. Shirley by his side. He listened to the house. His head leant up tight against it. Nothing but silence. He tried the door handle, expecting nothing, but was surprised when it opened. Pleasantly. Excellent. He flashed a quick smile at Shirley, and then pushed it open, keeping a careful eye on the darkness beyond. Nothing jumped out at him. No dog. That was good.

The door, wide enough for the two of them, they entered the house.

He slipped it closed behind them. "Five, you said?" she whispered.

He nodded.

"We need to do this *quiet*."

He smiled. He knew that. He tapped the rope. "Restrain first, then we decide."

Shirley nodded without speaking again. The two of them, at the foot of the stairs. Danny stopped and listened. Nothing. He had no way of knowing where any of them were. He looked around the shadows of the downstairs. Open plan living space, and a huge looking kitchen through a door to the left. He certainly didn't expect there to be a bedroom down there. So, he went up, slow. Trying not to make any noise on the wooden stairs.

The landing above, a runner of carpet down the middle of the floor to the doors. All closed except one. He edged to the open one and glanced around the corner. The bathroom.

Then a noise. A light flicked on under one of the doors. He snapped air into his lungs, and pulled back, retreating to the edge of the stairs and down to Shirley.

Watching as the door opened. The young woman from before—when he'd visited the house for the first time. Naked. She pulled the door half closed behind her as she yawned out, eyes a slit. Half awake.

She padded,, to the bathroom and in. Danny raised his eyebrows as this grown woman didn't close the door, listening as she peed, water splashing noises filling the hallway. Then it stopped and the silence returned. She padded back out to the hall and along to the bedroom.

Didn't wash her hands.

Nice arse though.

Danny waited. This had to be a family set up. But wandering naked in the middle of the night? She had to be in there on her own. The two brothers in different rooms. The parents elsewhere. He watched her close the door. Waved Shirley forward and took to the darkness of the hallway once again. The light under the door of the girl's room, extinguished. He stopped at the door and listened quietly. He could hear something … but he wasn't sure what. Pausing, a quick glance back to Shirley to make sure she was there, then he took the door handle and turned it, silently. He pushed it open, just a crack, and looked. In the shadows, he could see movement of silhouettes against the moonlight coming in from the far window.

Danny squinted. Waiting for his eyes to adjust to the light. She was there. He was half expecting her to be fingering one out in the bed … didn't expect her to have a boyfriend in there. But fine. He had plenty of rope—he glanced at Shirley's machete—and that, of course. No idea if the boyfriend was a part of it all or not. Whatever.

He pushed the door open slowly and slipped into the room. The two of them were too tied up in each other to be worried about him.

She was up. Riding him cowgirl. Hands on his chest, rocking back and forth.

Cunt said, "Who's your daddy?" like a complete jerk off. Fucking sounded old enough to be, too. Dirty fucker. He was probably some inbred hick from the local town. Some toothless urban farmer. Fucking *Giles*. Danny slipped around behind her, out of sight, while Shirley positioned herself at the door.

Danny came forward.

He grabbed the girl. One hand around her tits, the other over her mouth and he pulled her from the geezer. He unplugged like a phone that had been tripped over, and before he could call out, Shirley had her blade down, resting on his neck. "Not a word," she whispered. She looked to his hands, tied above his head, bound to the bedpost. "This fucker is already tied up and tied down," she hissed. A look to Danny. The bitch was flailing and kicking, but he was holding her tight, up off the floor, still behind her.

She managed to get her mouth out, and she chomped his fingers.

Danny pulled his hand away and pushed her to the floor. She landed in a crumpled heap, the sound of her body hitting the floor echoing around the inside of the whole house like the thing was made from balsa wood.

She looked up and Danny saw her draw air to scream, so he pulled his hand back and punched her in the nose. The skin on her face split open and her head snapped back, banging against the bed post behind her and knocking her out cold. She slumped naked to the floor.

Then a knocking came on the wall and the muffled shout, "Keep it down you two."

Danny looked at Shirley, frowning. Then they used the girl's underwear to gag her old man boyfriend. Tied her up like a hog.

Danny holding back vomit. This girl … the old man … her *old man*. What kind of fucked up shit was this?

———

Danny waited at the next door. Had one of the younger men in there, for sure. They'd heard through the wall, after all. Shirley smiled. That banging and such—he *had* to be alone. No way was that noise interrupting a night of passion with some tart from the pub. Danny wondered if she had, *you know*. He shook his thoughts away. Back to the task at hand. Checking for light under the door he saw nothing and so he opened it up a little.

Only a little.

Looked into the darkness beyond. Saw the bed. The curtains in the room were open and there was enough light to confirm that he was alone in the bed. That was something. He slipped in and went to the bed. The man in it was laying on his side, facing away from the door.

He said, "Not now, Ant. I'm trying to sleep."

What the fuck? Danny felt a slight turn in his stomach. This was too … *weird* … for words. He was going to find out what was going on, though. Before him … he raised Shirley's massive blade and hit the prone figure with the hilt of the machete on the side of the head. He let out a small grunt before his tense torso slumped under the covers.

Danny turned him onto his back. He was out cold. Then he tied his hands behind his back and gagged him. Just in case.

There were who … the wife? … mother? … even he wasn't sure now. Her and the other young man— the other son.

———

Danny pushed the door open to the master bedroom. The room darker than the other, but only a little. He could see the woman in the bed, alone, her husband in the other room fucking their daughter. *No.* That couldn't be it. That was far too disgusting for words. It had to be some fucked up group. A cult. Or something like that. Just all fucking each other and pretending to be a family. Holding visitors captive in the barn. Danny's grip tightened on the machete. Strapping them into milking machines. *Then murdering them.*

The woman in the bed turned and groaned out. She glanced up in the dark and saw the outline of Danny in the darkness. "Anton," she whispered. "Tha' you?"

She pulled the sheets from the bed. Spread her legs. "Make it quick," she said. "And don't wake the 'ouse."

Danny wanted to throw up. He strode across the room and to the side of the bed, where the woman opened her eyes. There was a second where she didn't seem to register that he was neither Anton, nor anyone else that was supposed to be there, when her eyes widened.

Danny pushed his hand over her mouth, stopping the noise from coming out. "Deviant motherfuckers," he muttered, pulling the pillow over her face and stopping her from screaming.

Shirley came in and bound her hands. They gagged her, too, before going to the last bedroom.

C H A P T E R   2 6

"So, I'm going to have to get you all to explain this to me. Like I'm thick, maybe?" Danny was standing in the kitchen doorway. Leant against the doorframe, Shirley on the far side of the room. Arse against the sink. She had the machete resting in her arms like a baby.

The five of them were tied, sitting at the kitchen table like some ghoulish fucking dinner party. All in the states of undress they were discovered in. Danny, after finding the second of the brothers, had worried less about noise when grabbing him and dragged them all down there. Tied them to the chairs and waited until all were awake to answer his questions.

The old man. The father, fucking the girl. His daughter. He nodded, slowly, like his head hurt. It probably did as Danny wasn't exactly gentle going down the stairs with any of them.

Shirley pulled the gag from him.

He stretched his mouth out and then his eyes met Danny's. "What do youse want?" he growled.

"I want you to explain all …" he waved his hand

over them, "… of this, to me."

"What?" he sighed.

Danny shook his head. "You don't understand my confusion?"

"No."

"Right," he whispered. "This …" he put his hands on the girl's bare shoulders. She flinched, pulling against the ropes that held her to the chair. "Who is this?"

"Jean," he said. There was an honest look of concern and worry on his face, like he really didn't know what the problem was.

"And who is Jean?" Danny said, a little impatient, tired already of having to lead him.

"My little girl."

Danny's stomach turned again. "Your daughter?"

"Yes," he replied, slowly.

"Why were you having sex with her?" Danny asked. He was trying not to lose his temper before he'd gotten the answer to the real question he had.

"I didn't fancy my wife tonight?" His voice rose on the last word, still confused.

"No," Danny said. He nodded at Shirley, and she replaced the gag. The look in the fucker's eyes of complete confusion.

Then she pulled the gag off the girl. She was crying and snotty. "Why are you doing this?" she barked.

Danny shook his head. "Why are you fucking your dad?" he snapped back.

Her bawling got louder. "I don't know what your problem is …"

Shirley put the gag back on. Took it from the mother.

"Youse cunt," she said.

"Nice," Danny said. "Perhaps you can shed some light on who is who at the table." He pointed to the first boy. "Yours?" She nodded. Pointing at Lewis, "And is he his?" She stared him down for a second, before shaking her head.

"No."

"And him." Pointed at the other boy.

"Not 'im either."

"And her?"

"She's ours."

"And where do you get donors from to make the others?"

"He only makes girls, see," she said in some pathetic defence.

Danny shook his head. "So, you lure in unsuspecting tourists to provide … samples … for you to make more?" She nodded, and Danny indicated to Shirley that the gag should go back up. "I'm only going to ask this once." He pulled the photo of his brother from his pocket and put it in the middle of the table. "What happened to him?"

The five of them all struggled to lean forward to see the photo. The girl just sat back. She clearly wasn't about to get involved. Then they started to look at each other. Some unspoken conversation going on. Then Lewis nodded for his gag to be removed. Shirley pulled it off.

The man sneered. "No idea what you're talkin' about," he said.

Danny nodded, poked out his bottom lip a little. "Like that is it?" he asked. "I see." He smiled, rounding the table as Shirley put the gag back on Lewis. He took her machete and walked around behind the five of them circling. He stopped at one of the boys. Seemed the best place. Then he brought the machete around and held it at the young man's neck. He paused there for a second. Lewis's eyes wide, and Maisie's full of tears.

Then Danny drew the sharp of the blade across his neck. Blood spat from the wound quickly, streaming out over the table in front of him as he struggled for freedom, jerking from side to side. Maisie screamed under the gag, thrashing to get free and help her son. Jean cried out, her brother cut open. Anton wailed like a baby, as if Tim was his lover and he was having the life cut from him.

Which he was. And he was.

Danny continued to stroke the blade back and forth, cutting into his flesh, the jagged edge of the steel at the hilt tearing the skin, as it drew through to the windpipe. Tim spluttering and coughing behind the gag as his throat slashed through, tears of flesh, chunks falling to the table as Danny jerked the blade to and fro. The boy shuddered and juddered as the blood flow slowed and the head started to tear free. The blade to the bone, the spine.

Danny was breathing air in and out, controlled. Tired, but filling with a sense of satisfaction at the kill. Head full of ways to kill these fucking freaks. The blade hit the bone, and he started to hammer against it.

Steel clanging on bone.

It didn't even register with Danny that the torso had stopped moving and the smell of iron that filled the room was the boy's blood on the outside of the body. And a little bit of wee, too, but that could have been any of them.

Finally, the blade parted the spine and holding his head by the hair, Danny lifted it aloft, like it was some sort of magical sword. Fat globs of viscera drooled from the neck hole. Stringing down to the corpse below like strawberry jam. Danny placed the head on the table.

"Now," he said. "You have forced me to ask again." He tapped the table near the photo with the tip of the blade. "What happened to him?"

There was a short silence in the room, and then the remaining four of them burst into life, apparently desperate to reveal the family secrets in exchange for their lives.

Danny waved his hands to calm them, and then Shirley went around the table removing all their gags, one at a time. "Now stay calm," Danny was saying, "let's all think this through and make sure we get this straight."

When the gags were all removed, he looked at the four of them, and asked, "So how did he end up here?"

"He was picked up after leaving the pub," Jean said.

"By?" Danny said.

"It was me," she continued. "I saw him leaving the pub and my mum said she needed someone to help her with a boy and I just thought …" She stopped speaking like she'd just realised that she was saying far too much. "I just brought him here, that's all. I didn't do nothing to him. Dropped him off and went back to the city."

Danny nodded along, "And then what?"

"I tried to make a baby," Maisie said quietly. "But he didn't want me."

"So, I put him on the machine," Anton continued.

Danny swallowed back the bile from his throat. He could see his poor naïve little brother getting fucked by the barmaid. Thinking he'll stick around … maybe get laid a bit more. Then picked up by this bitch. Promise of more tail no doubt. Maybe other things. Drugs? Who knows. Dragged back here and chained up in the barn, just like Richard. Told to fuck this cunt.

Then the machine.

Danny shook his head. "Then?"

"'E was a seedless fruit," Maisie said. It was all

Danny had not to leap across the table and cut her into little pieces right then.

"So, I fed him to Daisy," Lewis said.

After a long silence, Shirley asked, "Daisy?"

"My prize-winnin' pig. Good girl, she is."

Danny blinked.

C H A P T E R   2 7

Danny stared at the four of them for a moment, thinking. There was this static noise in his head, spinning and twirling, dancing like a firefly, unable to lay down on any one thing. The face of his brother in the centre of the thoughts, rolling around and around. He shook his head. "You." He pointed at Anton. "Let's get you up." He took Anton under the arms, hauling him to his feet. The chair dropped backward, clattering loudly to the floor.

Danny dragged him to the side of the kitchen, pushing him roughly to the side, as Shirley replaced the gags on the other three.

Danny handed her the machete. "If they so much as move … run them through. That'll slow them down." He shook his head.

"Please don't," Anton was wailing. "I didn't do nothing."

Danny slammed a fist into his stomach, tore the air from him and doubled him over. Spit dribbled from his mouth, out and down, onto the stone floor. "Shaddap," Danny barked. He righted the younger man and dragged him to the kitchen door, giving a cursory nod to Shirley, before dragging him out to the front door of the house.

He pushed him out, into the yard, and Anton dropped from his feet to his knees. Maybe he lost his footing, but more likely it was a tactic to slow down being taken to the barn. Danny moved to him and tried to pick him up, but he was flaccid. Lolling about like a squirmy sack of spuds. Danny let him drop to the floor, whining and pleading, and then stuck a boot into his torso. Anton cried out in pain, the sound of his voice filling the yard, and the sound of the pigs rising in the night. He bent down and grabbed Anton again, pulling him back to his feet. He stood this time. Tears on his face. His head hung in defeat. Danny pushed him along to the door of the barn.

"W-What are you going to do?" he cried out.

Danny opened the door. "We'll see." He pushed him in and over to where he'd found Richard. Kicked out the back of his knee and Anton dropped to the straw.

"I didn't do anything to your brother. I don't even recognise him."

"Not what you said a minute ago," Danny replied absently, looking around the barn. He spied the machine. What Richard had said it was for … what it did. His head dropped to the side. He continued looking around. Anton hadn't bothered trying to get back to his feet. His hands bound behind his back … and he looked far too foppish to be able to outrun Danny.

"I've got money," he pleaded. "I can pay you." He was staring at Danny, his eyes wild with fear.

Danny nodded, "That right." He went to the side wall and pulled a pair of shears from the straw. They would do. Then he returned to Anton. The boy kicked away trying to push himself across the floor of the barn and away, afraid of what Danny was going to do with the blades.

But Danny bent down and started to hack his pyjamas from his body, deftly, the speed of a seamstress. He pulled the shreds of material from him until he was naked as the day he was born. "Don't," he was muttering repeatedly. He kept moving around trying to face Danny.

Danny slapped him. "You think I wanna rape you?" he growled. Then he spat on the boy.

Anton shied away in fear. "I'll do anything," he whispered.

"Whatever," Danny snarled. He went to the machine. Pulled the thing through the straw closer to Anton. "So," he said. "How does this shit work?" He smiled at Anton. A little smugly, he thought. This close to retribution, and he was starting to feel a little better. "You put my brother on the machine, you're getting the machine." He flashed that smile again and then picked up the cylinder with the tube attached to the end. "Huh." He bent over Anton as he tried to squirm away and punched him in the nose. Blood shot from it as the cartilage below the skin cracked and snapped. Anton yelled out, his blood drooling down into his mouth. Head flopped back as he dropped prone to the straw.

"Fucking hell," Danny said, strapping the wank part of the machine to Anton, who did nothing more than lay, groaning on the floor. Danny turned to the machine and picked up the next bit. He looked at it. Another cylinder. This one was more … torpedo shaped. He sniffed it. Wished he hadn't. Fucking stupid thing to do.

Danny shook his head.

Bent forward and grabbed Anton's head. He stuffed the vibrating dildo into his mouth, stifling the grunts as he did, pushing it in and chipping his teeth.

He grabbed the duct tape from the machine shelf and wrapped it around Anton's head, sealing the vibrator in his mouth, around his head, sticking his hair down, around and around. Until Anton stared widely through slit gaps in the tape. The vibrator, now glued into his mouth, blood streaming from his nose. He could barely breathe through the tape. His nose was broken and swelling.

Then Danny turned and switched the machine on.

She roared into life and started to push and pull on his cock, the dildo started to vibrate against his teeth.

Anton curled backwards like he'd been electrocuted. Stiffening. He screamed from beneath the tape, head twitching to the side, blood spattering away to the already blackened straw of the last poor fucker to be there.

Danny shook his head and walked away. Back to the barn door. He glanced back to Anton, looked like he was spasming on the ground, twitching and twisting.

He closed the door and returned to the house.

To the kitchen, where Shirley still had the blade in her hand and the three of them just sat there. Maybe paralysed with fear. Unable to fight back ... or unwilling. Danny smiled to himself. Good. Compliance made it all the easier.

He looked at the three of them. "Who's next?"

Gagged, they all looked at him, terrified.

"Ah," he said. He went to the oldest of them, the man. Pulled the gag down. "So, you're Daddy, right?" Danny leant down from behind, his mouth close to the man's ear. "Who do you think should be next, hm?" Danny smiled. He could hear his breathing laboured in fear. "You, maybe?" The man twitched. He was too much of a coward to choose himself. "What about wifey?" Lewis flicked his head in her direction.

"Don't make me choose," he said.

"The daughter. I forget, she yours or not?" Danny actually *had* forgotten. He could smell the sweat running down Lewis's face. He was staring at his daughter. "Not that I think any of it matters ... not with this family dynamic." Danny straightened. "So, who's it to be? You, the wife, or the lover?"

Lewis's eyes were fixed on those of his wife's. She was staring back her look a mix of fear and incredulity.

"Are you going to choose the wife?" Danny asked quietly.

Lewis nodded slowly. Maisie screamed under her gag. Tears flooding quickly down her face.

Danny leant forward again, putting his lips close to Lewis's ears. "Say it," he said. Lewis shook his head. "Say it, or I'll cut your daughter's head off and make you fuck it."

"Maisie," he wailed. "Kill *Maisie*."

Maisie was bouncing in the chair, fear of Danny, hate and anger pointing straight at the fucked-up husband. He should have chosen himself. Any *real* man would have.

But Danny was a man of his word. He replaced the gag on Lewis and went around the table to Maisie, removing hers. He was kind of interested in what she had to say.

"You cunt," she barked. "You little pricked, hedgehog fucker. You mankey fuck southern bitch. You …" she paused for breath, then looked at her daughter. "… whore," she finished. Jean was just looking down at the table, tears dripping to the wood. Danny wondered if she was a little smarter than the rest of them and knew that all the pleading and bargaining was going to get them nowhere.

Danny pulled Maisie from the chair. She stood with him, willing, perhaps, to get from the room and the eyes of her husband.

Well, it wasn't that easy. Danny pushed her forward, folding her over the table. She landed, her face flat on the wood, close to Tim's head. She looked at the head for a second and then started to cry and wail. She struggled now, but Danny held her firm. His hand flat in the middle of the woman's back. She managed to turn her head and look the other way. Then she begged.

"Youse can 'ave anything youse want," she blubbed. "Money? Youse can fuck me."

Danny glanced to Shirley, standing, watching. He snorted. "I can fuck her," he echoed.

Shirley laughed. "Oh … good," she said dryly.

"Youse can fuck Jean," she said. "Everyone else 'as."

"You're really selling it." Danny held his hand out for the machete and Shirley handed it to him. He looked at Lewis, just once, quickly. A little wink. A *this is for you*, *for choosing her* wink. "Jean," he said.

She looked up.

"Watch," he said. Then he pulled the machete back and pointed it at her bottom region. He wasn't sure if he even cared where it went, but he knew it was appropriate to fuck her with it. He jammed the machete forward into the woman. It bounced once, hitting something hard. She screamed out in pain. Danny probed slightly to the left and tried again. This time, the sharp end of the blade slipped through her clothing into her flesh. In with some ease. She screamed out, but froze up as the blade went in easier than he thought it would have. But still, she didn't move.

"Anal?" he said. Looking at the machete a good eight or nine inches were inside her and she didn't seem to be squealing out in pain or writhing like he'd slashed her open. She was breathing short sharp breaths. Danny looked at Lewis. "She doesn't normally take it up the jacksy, does she?"

Lewis shook his head.

Danny nodded. He glanced to Jean to make sure she was still watching, which she was, and then he twisted the blade.

The steel spun around in her arsehole with enough ease that he could turn it and turn it, grating off her fleshy butt fat, and blending her insides. She grunted like a prize porker, and lurched trying to move away from the blade, but folded over the table, she couldn't. She started to choke, blood coming from her mouth, spitting out over the table at Jean, and then she made this high-pitched squeak.

Danny continued to stir her insides like he was making a cake as the woman's rolls and attempts at freedom became twitches. The squeaking stopping, and the woman stilled. But Danny continued. The dull sound of steel on bone, like a spoon on the side of a teacup as he went around and around in her arse slurry, slow, watching Jean cry and gag, staring into her dead mother's eyes. Watching as Lewis refused to look. Even with Shirley holding his head, trying to force him to watch his wife be stirred, he tried to fight her to look away.

Danny smiled.

"You're next."

C H A P T E R   2   8

Danny pulled Lewis to his feet. His head thrashed from side to side as he tried to stop Danny from taking him anywhere.

Danny held the blade to his throat and the man stopped thrashing. The smell of pee overrode the smell of copper and iron in the room, and from behind Lewis, Danny saw the look change on Jean's face as her father and sometimes lover—or vice versa—pissed himself. Danny drew him back from the table, fighting around the chairs.

"Come on Lewis, m'boy. Be a man. Just for once in your wretched snivelling little life, be a man." He smiled at Shirley as he man-handled Lewis out of the house.

To the yard.

Into the darkness.

———

Daisy stood watching. There had been quite some comings and goings over the last while. That man and the woman. Then the man came out with the master's son. Now the man and the master approached.

Daisy made some pigly assumption that the master was going to feed her the man. She watched, but as they got closer, the master seemed to be bound … tied perhaps. She oinked playfully. Hungrily. A glance to her brother. She'd wished he was asleep, and then whatever morsels of food would be hers, but he was awake. Standing at the back of the pen, watching, distrusting.

That was okay. She'd show him it was all okay. The master came to the side of the pen, but the man was holding the master's weapon to his own neck. That was probably something other things should be concerned with and not her, because she was a hungry pig and concerned little else.

She heard her brother shit a little.

Maybe that was what he was doing up against the back of the pen.

"Please don't kill me," the master was saying. She could feel his distress. Whatever was happening out there must have been bad. But she was starving and wanted it to play out quicker, so she could eat.

The pen opened and the master was shoved in. He dropped to his knees into the mire of pig stuff they enjoyed walking about in so much. He turned his head and looked at the man. Master didn't seem concerned about her and her brother.

Then the man closed the gates.

He said, "Go on then."

Daisy didn't know what words meant. She did, however, recognise the smell of fear on the master. She shuffled to him, closer. His whipping hands were bound behind him, and he was no threat. He saw her coming closer and tried to move away, falling from his knees into the mess, and making a noise like … like the dinners he brought did sometimes.

Daisy tried to smile. A pig smile is quite the thing to behold. It looks, quite frankly, terrifying.

The master squirmed away, but between the smell and the sound and the fear and the piss, Daisy came to realise that the man was the master now, and this man, the old master, was nothing more than dinner.

Then she opened her maw and tore into his leg. Just below the knee, her teeth sank into the softened flesh, and she pulled the skin and the flesh from the bone and yanked it from him. His screaming filled the air. His blood in her mouth. She chewed with glee on the flesh of the man, swallowing it back quickly, before her brother got involved. In again, to the same spot, her powerful maw chewing down and crushing the bones like a machine.

———

Lewis howled as the pig chewed his leg off with ease. Danny curled back slightly, sickened by the sight. But the way the pig went for him … nothing Lewis had said had been a lie. These pigs are man-eaters. Jesus *fucking* Christ.

Just before he turned away, the second pig had

taken one arm, the first had the other and they were pulling at him in some macabre tug of war, as Lewis, leaking gore over the mud, screamed and screamed and screamed.

Then he broke like a Christmas cracker, each pig winning, taking an arm each as Lewis, a head, torso, and leg lay, mumbling in the mud, lost to his insanity, taken by shock and pain.

"Nice," Danny muttered, watching the two pigs gleefully chow down on the arms they now had.

He returned to the barn and pulled the door open. Looked in on Anton. He was laying on the floor motionless.

Danny went to the machine and stopped it. He was still expecting him to be writhing around in pain. He looked down at him, naked on the straw. The blood in his nose, blocked and dried, and his mouth filled with liquid. The vibration in his mouth had shattered his teeth, and between the blood in there and the tape, he'd drowned in his own blood, unable to breathe through his nose.

Shame.

Danny wasn't sure he was finished with him. Not yet. He sighed. Left the barn and returned to the house.

C H A P T E R   2 9

Jean was snorting back snot and tears, head drooped down, trying not to look at the corpses of her mother and brother. His head staring into some abyss just off her left shoulder, and her mother, raped by a machete blade.

The room, full of squalid heat, ripe and mouldy.

Danny and Shirley stood on the other side of the table watching her silently. Danny holding her hand, gently squeezing it every now and then. "So, what to do with the lure?" Danny whispered. It wasn't quiet enough for Jean not to hear. In fact, it, like everything else, was going to make her feel worse about the situation.

"The lure," Shirley repeated. "Yeah."

Danny nodded at the contents of the table. "Sorry about all this. I know it's not what you signed up for."

She pulled her hand from him, snatching it back, before moving it down and grabbing his crotch. "You can make it up to me later."

He glanced at her, a wry little smile on her face. Dirty cow. He smiled back. "That can be arranged."

Then Jean looked up to the two of them, finally managing to spit her gag out. "So, what are you going to do with me?" she said, through wet sobs.

"Take you back to town, I guess. Pay for what you've done." Shirley's voice was level, but with a sinister tinge to it.

Danny glanced at her. She really was on board. Nice. He leant in a little closer. "What's the plan?" he whispered, this time low enough that she couldn't hear.

"Get her up." Her smile flashed brighter for a second. "You'll see."

———

Danny pushed the key into the ignition of the flatbed truck parked down the side of the farmhouse. The key turned, and the engine sparked into life. He looked through the window of the vehicle to Shirley, standing with Jean. They'd demanded the keys, and Jean was pleased to tell them where they were, as long as she was getting a free lift into town.

At least, that was what she thought she was getting.

Danny dropped out of the vehicle, to the mud. "Got petrol and everything."

Shirley smiled. She roughly took Jean's elbow and led her towards the truck, but as they got to the door, she veered towards the back. Jean yelped a little, and then must have realised she was riding in the back, moving without putting up a fight.

Shirley took her to the back, and Danny came up behind her. He put his hand on her shoulder. No words. Just an action enough to say that he was there, and she wasn't about to get away. Not now. Not if she tried.

Shirley took the chain she'd gotten from the barn and wrapped it around the tow bar of the flatbed. Locking it off. Then she and Danny pulled Jean around to the back of the vehicle and secured the chain around her ankles. Chained together. Her hands still tied behind her back. Her crying getting louder as they did.

But she was resigned to it. She didn't fight or struggle. She just wept and moaned and sobbed as she realised what they were doing. And when they stood next to her. The fumes chugging from the exhaust at their feet, she didn't even raise her head. No protests. Just the sad acceptance. She was going back to town.

To pay for what she'd done.

"Mind if I drive?" Shirley asked. "You seem to have done all the driving so far."

"Shotgun," Danny replied, dryly.

The two of them got into the flatbed and when Shirley applied the brake, putting it in gear, Jean was bathed in the red glow of the lights from the back. Her head was up now. Tears streaked her face, and in that red glow, it looked like she was crying blood.

Shame.

Then Shirley hit the accelerator, and the vehicle moved off.

———

Jean's legs jerked from under her, and in that split second, she was in the air, everything felt okay. She felt like she was flying. Up. Away. Soaring. Then she hit the ground like a body bag thrown from a truck. The weight of the vehicle pulling her by her legs, her first thought was that her hips would break and she might snap in half. The mud thrashing against the side of her body as the truck crossed the yard. Everything hurt. She could hear nothing, except this continual grinding sound. She wasn't sure what it was, but the truck noise changed, and she realised it had left the yard, and she was about to, as well.

Onto the dried, hard surface of the track that passed for a road, from the actual road to the yard. Suddenly Jean felt like she was being beaten with rocks. Pummelled from all sides, her head bouncing off the dried dirt. Stone cutting into her. Her hands behind her as she rolled onto her front, her back, and back again. Twisting and burning. Breaking fingers, and wrists.

Then the noise changed again, and the flatbed turned onto the road. Jean joined it in a moment, a split-second passing, a second of realisation of what was about to happen, and she was on tarmac, increasing in speed.

On her side, the burning was the first thing. She felt like the side of her body was on fire, so she rolled. The flash of relief as she rolled onto her back, gone as the burning returned.

Subsiding to pain as the flesh began to flay from

190 | A s h   E r i c m o r e

her body.

———

Daisy watched the master's daughter being pulled from the yard. Shame. She looked tasty. She put her trotters on the master's chest and stuck her snout into the cavity where his guts used to be. Her brother had taken the liver. Shame. She enjoyed the iron taste of that. But it was okay. She'd stored a little something for later. In the corner. She'd hidden it in the mud.

C H A P T E R   3 0

Danny jumped from the vehicle and went to the rear. Looked at what was left of the girl. It was shaped like a human sized chicken drumstick. Just wetter. The arms torn off somewhere down the road, the head more of a stump than a head now. He nodded appreciation of the kill. Shirley watching him through the back window. She saw the nod and killed the engine.

Got out and rounded to him. "You sure you want to do it like this?"

Danny nodded. He looked from the corpse—what was left of it—to the church. Then the time. It was still the early hours. Plenty of time to get out of Dodge.

The two of them hot footed back to the pub. Let themselves in and returned to the room. Richard was still asleep or unconscious, or whatever. They worked quickly and silently, packing their clothes and making sure they'd left no obvious evidence.

There was physical evidence, sure, but neither of them had been in trouble with the law before, their DNA and such wasn't going to be on record. Shirley slung the bag over her shoulder, and then they left.

Richard still sleeping.

Out on the road, they walked with some haste. When a car was coming, they'd slip into the bushes or behind a tree to remain incognito. Danny took Shirley's hand. "Thank you," he said. "I don't think I could have done it without you."

She smiled. It was nice of him to say so. But she was sure he'd have found a way. They walked in silence for a few minutes. Then she said, "So, are we a couple now, and not just a screw?"

Danny laughed. "Yeah, I guess you want to meet my mum?"

"How will she take it … all this?"

"You think I'm going to tell her?" Danny shook his head. Oh, no. That was going to be a job for someone else.

The two of them reached the bike after an hour or so of walking. Just where they'd left it. On the road near the farm.

They prepped the bike for a drive, Danny checking the time. Then they rode away from Crumbsbottom inthe opposite direction. Stopping in the next village, where in the centre of the square, like the last town was a phone box. Called the police.

Danny told them where Richard was. Where Jean was. And where the farm was, before hanging up and leaving. The police would never know it was them. Richard wouldn't be able to give them much, not in the state he was in. Not enough, anyway.

And Shirley wrapped her arms around him and squeezed.

P R O L O G U E

Two dead in the kitchen, one in the barn." The uniform looked at Havelstan, as he shuffled wanting nothing more than to pass this all over to the detective and fuck off.

Havelstan nodded, thumbing the notes into his phone. "Anything else?"

"The puke over to the side of the barn is ours. Forensics should ignore it."

Havelstan looked over his glasses at the man. "Yours?"

"No, Johnson." He waved in the direction of the green officer. Green in more ways than one.

Havelstan swallowed back his words. He wanted to reprimand them, but it was hardly worth it. Between this and the bits found in the village, it looked like some sick spree kill. Weird though. Who breaks into a farm and kills the occupants in such a fashion? The machine in the barn. Beheading? All the cars down the side of the barn?

Very weird.

———

The flashing lights looked very pretty. Daisy stood, watching. There were all these new people. She wondered if she was going to get to taste any of them. She glanced at her brother, fat and full of the master. They needed a new master now. Theirs was gone. Well …

… almost.

She looked content that her brother was asleep and content with his fatness, before going to the side of the sty and pushing her trotter through the mud, to look at her prize again. Saving it for later. She could barely wait. Wanting to taste it. Lewis's dead eyes stared back from the mud, his head rolling lightly with the touch of the pig. Yes.

Most tasty.

A B O U T   T H E
A U T H O R

Ash Ericmore lives in Kent in England. By the seaside. He rarely leaves the house. A hermit by any other name, he lives on a council estate.
Hiding from everyone.

Seen once in shadow on a wildlife documentary, many dubious articles have been offered in attempts to prove the existence of Ericmore, including anecdotal claims of observations as well as dubious video and audio recordings, photographs, and casts of his monstrous footprints.

He is founder of the Ericmorean Church of Splatterology.

He can rarely identify an arse from an elbow.

You can find him at www.ashericmore.com.

Dawn Shea is an author and half of the publishing team over at D&T Publishing. She lives with her family in Mississippi. Always an avid horror lover, she has moved forward with her dreams of writing and publishing those things she loves so much.

Follow her author page on Amazon for all publications she is featured in.

Follow D&T Publishing at their website, www.dt-publishing.com, or search for their Facebook Group

Or email here: **dandtpublishing20@gmail.com**

Farm Animals by Ash Ericmore

Cover by Ash Ericmore

Edited by Tasha Schiedel

Formatting by Ash Ericmore

www.ingramcontent.com/pod-product-compliance
Lightning Source LLC
Chambersburg PA
CBHW051954220626
47052CB00004B/934